A LOVE TO HAVE AND TO HOLD

LINDA FORD

CHAPTER 1

MONTANA TERRITORY, 1884

*W*alker's legs buckled. He caught himself before he fell. He wiped his eyes. Shimmering shapes ahead made him squint to focus. Buildings. A town. He stumbled forward. A steeple on the nearest building pointed heavenward. *Thank You, God. I made it.* He staggered the last few paces and collapsed on the steps of the church. From inside, came the sound of a piano and ladies singing in harmony. *Amazing grace, how sweet the sound.*

Yes, Lord, it was Your amazing grace and love that brought me to safety.

The music stopped. The door behind him was ajar, and he heard bits and pieces of a conversation.

"He'd like to court you."

A second voice answered. "I don't want to encourage

him." Walker missed a few words from the first speaker. Then the second person spoke again. "I'm not interested in marriage, but even if I was, it would not be with a penniless, homeless cowboy."

Walker figured that about described him. Not that he was looking for a wife. Nope. Besides, this wasn't the first young lady to speak her mind about poor cowboys. Dianne had taught him a lasting lesson on the matter. Now he had other things on his mind. Fog filled his brain, and he couldn't remember what his plans were. Wavy lines distorted the world around him. He leaned back, closed his eyes, and waited for the weakness to pass.

A hand touched his shoulder. The scent of wild flowers wafted into his senses.

"Mister, you look to be in need of help."

He couldn't answer.

"Wait here. I'll get my pa."

A different voice spoke. "Is he okay while you do that? I need to check on the children." The speaker seemed eager to be away.

A soft chuckle. "I don't think he'll be going anyplace soon."

Footsteps faded away. Walker's head echoed with the urgent beat of his heart.

Moments later a man's voice spoke, and there was a gentle touch on his shoulders. "You're in safe hands."

Walker squinted in an attempt to bring the face into focus. A kindly looking man with dark brown hair and steady gray eyes. Beside him, a young lady with similarly colored hair but brown eyes whose brow wrinkled in concern. He managed to take them in before his vision again blurred.

"Let's get him into the house." The man urged Walker to his feet, holding him as he swayed. With one person on either side of him, he was guided across a patch of grass and into a kitchen. He was lowered to a chair by the table.

"Mister," the man asked, "are you sick?"

Walker struggled to find the strength to talk. "Weak. Thirsty." He touched his head. "Got a bump here." The robber had hit him with the butt of his gun.

"I'll have a look." Walker flinched as the man parted his hair and examined the wound. "You have a goose egg, but it doesn't look serious. I expect it will hurt for a few days."

"Here, drink this." The young lady held a cup of cold water to his lips, and he drank eagerly. She hastened to bring him a bowl of soup and fed it to him spoonful by spoonful. He would have protested, but he didn't have the strength or the will. Slowly he began to feel his body. His brain started to clear.

The man sat opposite him. "Welcome to Glory, Montana Territory. Allow me to introduce myself. I'm the preacher, Jacob Kinsley. This is my daughter, Josephine." Another woman entered the room, with two children in tow. "This is Mrs. Norwood and her children, Blossom—"

A sweet looking little girl he thought might be about three.

"And Donny."

The boy could be five or six. Marshall wasn't good at

judging children's ages. But there was no mistaking the bright curiosity in the child's eyes.

Miss Josephine placed a cup of fragrant coffee before him. "Can you manage to drink it on your own, or do you need help?"

He recognized her voice as the one who had spoken against penniless cowboys. "I'll manage. Thank you." His self-respect had returned, but he soon discovered he needed to use both hands to lift the cup to his mouth. The hot drink served to revive him.

The preacher nodded. "I see you're feeling a bit better. Can you tell us what happened to you?"

"I was robbed. The scoundrel hit me on the head before he took my horse and saddle and all my supplies. Left me to perish."

"You proved him wrong, I'd say."

"If I hadn't found this place when I did, he might have succeeded." He'd been fighting the weakness of his body all morning. "It would have been so easy to stop putting one foot in front of the other." His world had narrowed down to that simple act.

"How many days since you were robbed?"

"Not sure but seems like it was five days. I've been wandering around, trying to find help since then."

A collective gasp came from the adults, and the little boy's eyes widened with admiration as he leaned on the corner of the table and watched Walker.

"Five days?" The preacher shook his head. "How did you survive?"

"Mostly I think I went in circles. Couldn't get my bearings." The blow to his head had left him dizzy and disoriented. "Yesterday, I found the road. I could see signs that the river was nearby, but I didn't have the strength to make it to the river and back. I hoped if I stayed on the road, someone would find me."

"You didn't encounter any homes?"

"I passed a homesteader's shack a couple days ago." He wasn't sure of the time frame any more than he was certain the place hadn't been born in the wanderings of his mind. "Didn't seem to be anyone home." He couldn't remember if he'd knocked on the door or not. One thing he was certain of. "I couldn't bring myself to take anything. Even being hungry doesn't make stealing right."

"God certainly had His hand on you."

"Preacher, I couldn't agree more."

"Now, you'll be needing somewhere to rest and recover your strength. Turns out I have just the place."

"Pa?" It was Miss Josephine. "What do you have in mind?"

"We'll put a cot in the addition." He held up a hand to forestall his daughter's objection. "I know it's not finished, but the walls are up, the roof is almost shingled. It will provide shelter."

"Yes, Pa."

"With your ma away tending to Mrs. Smith, I'll be counting on you."

"Of course."

"I can help," Mrs. Norwood offered.

Miss Josephine patted the woman's shoulder. "I will gladly accept help, but Ma would have my hide if I let you do too much. You need to rest and regain your strength."

Mrs. Norwood sighed. "It seems to be taking forever."

"There's no rush." Miss Josephine turned back to her father. "I'll help set up a place."

She and her father left. Young Donny remained at the table, studying Walker.

Walker grinned. "Do I look that bad?"

Donny nodded. "You's covered with dust, and your hair is pokey." He raised spread fingers to his head to indicate what he meant.

"Donny, mind your manners," the child's ma said.

Donny ducked his head. "Sorry, mister."

"No offense taken. I expect I am rather a mess, but I'll tell you, I'm mighty glad to be alive."

Mrs. Norwood breathed an "Amen." She raised her voice to speak to Walker. "You couldn't have found your-self in a better place. The Kinsleys are hospitable and will help you get back on your feet."

"I'm afraid I have nothing to offer them in exchange. I'm a poor, penniless cowboy without even a horse and saddle to my name."

"That won't make an ounce of difference."

Walker nodded. It might not matter to the preacher, but he was certain it mattered a lot to the preacher's daughter. Not that Walker cared. He only wanted to regain his strength, find a way to earn enough money to buy another horse and outfit, and then proceed with his plans.

* * *

JOSIE HELPED her pa set up a cot in the unfinished addition. "Pa, how long do you think he'll be here?" She spread out bedding as she spoke.

"As long as he needs to be. God has a plan in bringing him to us, and we don't want to miss out on what the good Lord has in store. Do we?"

"No, Pa." Her tone must have said more than she intended, because Pa stopped pushing aside pieces of lumber to study her.

"This is the reason we need the addition—so we can provide a place for the sick, the injured, and destitute. We can give them shelter and succor."

That's what the room down the hall was supposed to do, but it would be some time before Stella and her children could leave.

Pa continued. "Is there some reason you don't want him here? Is it because your mother is away? I have every confidence you can handle this. You're very capable."

"I don't mind the work." It was the man's words about not being able to bring himself to steal food even when he was hungry that twisted inside her stomach. Sometimes a person had to steal to survive.

"He's a fine looking fellow," Pa said, still watching her to see her reaction to his words.

"I suppose he is, though he could use some water to wash with and some clean clothes." Even in his disheveled state she couldn't help but note the man's dark blond hair, his piercing blue eyes, and the firmness of his chin.

Pa chuckled. "Josie, my dear daughter, someday a young man is going to make you forget your past and make you want to march into the future."

"Pa, you know I already have plans for my future."

Pa shook his head, his mouth drawn back in a slight frown. "Your plans sound lonely to me."

"I love sewing, and I see ladies as they come to order gowns and things." Though since they'd moved to Montana Territory, she didn't see many. "Soon I'll have enough money to buy a sewing machine, and then I'll set up business in a little shop." She'd be independent and self-sufficient, with her future secure.

"There's more to life than making money."

They'd had this discussion before. She'd explained it wasn't about the money. It was about security. But Pa insisted her only security was in trusting God.

"I can trust God and do my part as well." She stepped back and studied the room. Now that Pa had moved aside the lumber, she could see how dirty the floor was. "I better sweep up the sawdust."

"I'll bring out a stand and some water so he can wash." Pa chuckled. "He does have several layers of trail dust on him." He headed for the doorway. "I expect you can find something for him to wear in Ma's things."

"I'll look." Ma kept a good supply of clothes and bedding to be shared with those in need who came across their threshold.

A little later, she hurried back with what she'd found. Pa had warm water and a washstand ready and escorted Walker into the room.

"It's not much, but it's a place for you to stay until you get back on your feet." Pa said.

"I appreciate your hospitality."

"God put us all here at this time and place for His purposes," Pa said. "May each of us cooperate with His plans as He reveals them to us. Now, I see Josie has found you some clean clothes."

Josie laid the items out on the bed. "Not much, but they'll do until I can get those things washed."

"Thank you." Walker chuckled. "Young Donny informed me that I looked a tad dirty." His blue eyes met Josie's gaze.

She wondered at the challenge she detected.

Then he spoke, directing his words at her. "As a penniless, homeless cowboy, I am grateful for every kindness." His gaze held hers.

"We'll leave you to get cleaned up, then please join us in the kitchen. Josie is preparing dinner." Pa left the room.

Josie wondered at the familiarity of the words the visitor spoke then remembered she'd said them in the church just before they discovered Walker on the step. She returned his hard stare with one of her own. "You overheard me speaking to Stella."

"I did."

They'd been talking about the latest cowboy to hang around. Bart had been sharing Sunday dinners at Ma's invitation and then calling again and again in the hopes of getting Josie to go walking with him. But she'd vowed to never again be so poor she wouldn't know where the next meal was coming from nor if she would be without a roof over her head or a place to sleep. "I have my reasons for my stand."

"It matters not to me."

"Then why did you bring it up?"

He shrugged. "Maybe I found it an offensive way to judge a man."

"Not near as offensive as poverty is." She hurried from the room before he replied. He had no idea—not even her adopted family did—of her fears and shame at how she'd been forced to live before she joined the Kinsley family at age twelve. Ma and Pa knew a bit about what she'd done, but if any of them learned the whole truth they would condemn her.

Would she ever be able to put her past behind her?

CHAPTER 2

*T*here was no door to the room, but someone had hung a blanket over the opening, and Walker pulled it across to provide some privacy. He stripped off his clothes, waving away the cloud of dust that rose from them. Like Donny said, he was dirty. He washed as best he could in the basin the preacher had provided, but he'd give anything to find the river and submerse himself in the water. He'd do so at the first opportunity.

In the meantime…he donned the clothes. The brown pants were short as were the sleeves on the paler brown shirt, but he wasn't complaining.

He should not have judged Miss Josie's comments and would apologize when he saw her.

He rinsed dirt from his hair and combed it. The scoundrel who robbed him had even taken his hat. That was about as low as a skunk could get in Walker's opinion. There was no mirror, but he didn't need one to know slicking his hair down was useless. It would spring into waves as soon as he withdrew the comb. Ma had told him it made him even more handsome, but then he suspected she was a little bit prejudiced. It was her love for him and his for her that had him on this journey.

"Dinnertime," the preacher called.

"And I'm as ready as I'm going to be." At least the thief hadn't taken his boots. That would have been the last straw. If he'd tried, Walker would likely be dead of a gunshot wound by now. He took the sleeve of his dusty shirt and wiped his boots then pulled them on and returned to the kitchen.

"Sit there." The preacher indicated the chair at his right, and Walker sat. The chair across from him was empty. Mrs. Norwood sat next to it with the little girl beside her. Beyond them were several empty chairs.

Miss Josie put a tureen of soup in the middle of the table and added a pile of biscuits before she took the chair across from Walker.

Donny sat next to Walker and continued to study him.

"Mind your manners, son," his mother said, and the boy turned his attention to his plate.

Walker leaned toward the boy. "Do I look better?" he murmured.

Donny nodded. "Smell better too."

"Donny!" His mother looked ready to collapse.

Walker burst out laughing. "I 'spect I do." He heard the preacher's stifled chuckle and glanced across to where Miss Josie sat. He drew upright at the caution in her eyes. Did she think he would judge a child for an innocent remark? "Kids are nothing if not truthful," he said, smiling to indicate he wasn't offended.

She flicked her eyelids, but he couldn't tell if it was in acceptance or warning.

"I'll ask the blessing." The preacher's words drew Walker's attention from the young lady.

Walker bowed his head.

"Father above, we thank You for Your many blessings. We have food and shelter, and You've seen fit to bring this young man into our care. In all things, we give You thanks. Amen."

Walker felt blessed by the man's prayer, but he could think of no way to say so. And then the opportunity was gone as Miss Josie filled bowls with thick, creamy vegetable soup, and biscuits were passed around the table. He tasted the soup. Delicious. The biscuits were light.

"Good food." He nodded to Josie. Wondered at the caution in her eyes. It might be because he was poor and homeless, but why should that matter to her unless she thought he meant to take advantage of their hospitality?

"I'll find a way to pay for my meals," he said with enough firmness to make her blink. He studied her a moment longer. She wore a blue shirtwaist, the color of a warm summer sky. Too bad the warmth didn't extend to her brown eyes.

"Our hospitality is free," the preacher said. "Now tell us about yourself, Walker. Where are you from, and where are you going?"

"I'm originally from Texas. My father and uncle owned a ranch there, but they parted ways and sold the ranch."

Donny edged forward. "I'm gonna own a ranch some-day. Was it a big one? Who bought it?"

"Son." His mother sounded weary, and Walker gave her further study. She was pale. Her dark blue dress hung from her too-thin frame.

"It's okay," Walker assured the woman. He squeezed Donny's shoulder. "It was only a small ranch, and some neighbors bought it. Me and my folks moved on. We settled in Kansas. My pa died three years ago, and Ma passed last year. Before she died, I promised her I'd look up my uncle. She said the last they heard from him he was in Montana Territory near a place called Bella Creek."

"You're almost there. It's a good day's travel north of here," the preacher said.

"I'll be on my way as soon as I can buy a horse." But thanks to the robbery, he was flat broke with no prospects of a job. Perhaps a nearby ranch would hire him and provide horse and tack until he could afford to buy his own.

"No need to rush away," the preacher said.

Donny squirmed. Walker could tell he wanted to speak but didn't want to interrupt.

"What is it?" he asked the boy.

"Does your uncle own a ranch? Are you going to work for him?"

"I don't know whether or not he owns a ranch, but as to working for him…I kind of planned to keep moving north. I hear Canada is beautiful, and there are big ranches always looking for someone to hire. Or maybe I'll just keep moving north all the way to Alaska." He glanced about the table. "That's probably a whole lot more about me than you expected to hear."

"No," the preacher said. "Just about the right amount. I wish you God's best in your journey."

"Thanks."

The meal ended, and the preacher rose. "I need to get that addition finished while I have a chance." He paused. "Say, you could help me, if you wanted and when you're feeling better. I could surely use an extra pair of hands. I'll give you room and board plus a small salary in exchange for your work. What do you say?"

It was on the tip of Walker's tongue to say an immediate yes, but he saw the wariness in Miss Josie's eyes. "There's something I need to say to your daughter before I give you my answer."

Her eyes narrowed, and he swallowed hard. He would sooner speak his apology in private, but he must say what he had to say, whether in private or public.

"I apologize for judging your comment about poor, homeless cowboys. It wasn't my business, nor did I have the right to make it so. I fear I have offended you. I'm sorry. I'd like to help your pa, but I won't unless you can assure me you forgive me and that you are comfortable with me being here." It was one of the longest speeches he'd ever made. Seems he'd been robbed of more than his belongings… He'd also lost his usual brevity of speech.

She shifted her gaze to a spot beyond his left ear. Her eyes filled with a darkness that sucked the moisture from his mouth. Was she afraid of something? Of him?

* * *

Josie knew she had to say the right words, but forgiveness came hard for her. Both giving it and receiving it. He wanted her to be comfortable with him being there. But she wasn't. Nor could she say why. Perhaps because he had overheard her statement about cowboys, and it allowed him to see more of her than she usually allowed others to see. But he had admitted he was wrong in judging why she would say such a thing.

He would never know how deep her fear of having nothing was. Even deeper was her dread of having people know what she'd done because she'd had nothing.

"Josie." Pa spoke quietly.

She brought her gaze to Walker's. "I don't object to you staying. Pa could use the help."

Walker's eyes narrowed. "Does that mean you forgive me?"

She forced a smile to her lips. "I suppose it does." How often she had wondered if forgiveness would be so readily given to her if people knew the truth about her. Ma and Pa had said her past didn't matter to them, but then they were far more charitable than most and didn't know everything she'd done.

"Good. Good. Walker, why don't I show you what I'm in the midst of doing?" Pa led the man from the room, and Josie's shoulders relaxed.

"I'll help clean the kitchen." Stella began to gather up the dirty dishes. She gave Blossom a handful of silverware. "Take that to the dishpan."

Blossom did so. "I 'elp."

Josie grinned as she took the items. "Thank you."

"I'm going to help the men." Donny strutted out.

Josie waited until the door closed behind him then looked at Stella, and they both chuckled.

Stella pulled a chair to the cupboard so she could sit while drying dishes.

Before they were done, Josie could see Stella struggled with fatigue, and Blossom fussed at her side.

"Time to tuck your little one in for a nap. You rest with her."

"I hate to be so weak, but I can't seem to help it."

"You'll get strong again." Josie's sister, Flora, and Kade, who was now Flora's husband, had found Stella near death, her children also sick and weak, and had brought them to the parsonage to be cared for. As Ma said, it would take time for Stella to recover from such an experience. In the meantime, she was safe and welcome here.

The room grew quiet with Stella's departure. Sounds of muted male conversation came from the addition. Josie stilled to listen to the voices.

Pa was speaking. "Sorry to hear about your folks. It's hard to be alone in the world."

"I've had a year to get used to it."

Josie moved to the open window and unashamedly listened to the conversation.

"You're young to be without family except for an uncle you seem to have lost contact with."

"I'm twenty-four. I was twenty-one when Pa passed away. I had a job freighting in Missouri, but when I learned of his death, I went home to help Ma. She wasn't strong, so I moved her into town and got a job at the feed store. I stayed with her until the end."

Josie didn't move away. There was something about Walker's loyalty to his mother that tugged at her heart. If someone had cared for her like that...

Of course, she now had the Kinsleys, and she would forever be grateful to them.

"Not all sons are as loyal as you were."

Josie's eyes stung at the pain in Pa's voice. The Kinsley son, Josh, had disappeared. And he was their own flesh and blood, not adopted like all six girls.

Pa continued. "I have a son I haven't seen in two years. We moved here in the hopes of locating him."

"I'm sorry. That's got to hurt."

Pa nodded. "It does some. I continually ask God to help us find him or for Josh to find us."

"You have my sympathy."

Pa continued. "I have faith that we will find him. It seems your faith has survived the trial of losing your parents."

The men came 'round the corner, and Walker leaned against the bare walls.

Josie couldn't help but smile. The man's pose was confident, but his too-short pants and shirt sleeves that ended long before his wrists provided a different picture.

He continued to tell Pa about his life. "Losing my parents was hard but not as hard as the break up and selling of the ranch. I could never understand what happened. We were a family. Pa and Uncle Paul were partners. I always thought I would follow in their boots and run the ranch with them. We always talked about it, so I know it wasn't simply in my head. Then it ended, and no one ever offered an explanation though I asked numerous times until Pa said there was nothing to say. It just *was*. Ma wouldn't say anything until on her deathbed, then she told me to find Uncle Paul and say there were no hard feelings. Makes me wonder if my uncle did something like…I don't know. I've thought of it a lot over the years and can't come up with anything. Did he steal from my parents? Kiss my ma? Cheat? Or did one of my parents do something to offend him? I simply don't know. Maybe I never will."

Donny stood beside Walker and imitated his pose.

Josie smiled at the picture of the two.

Then Walker dropped his hand to the boy's shoulder, and Donny grinned widely, pleased at this small gesture of acknowledgment.

Josie's eyes stung with tears that got no further than the back of her eyes. She'd long ago grown adept at keeping tears at bay. She was about Donny's age when she was orphaned. If her uncle had shown the least bit of affection things might have been different, but he made it clear she was a nuisance and a burden. She recalled his words.

"Only thing you're good for is pretending to be an innocent kid." The problem was, that's exactly what she was until she had followed her uncle's directions so often that she was trapped in his way of life.

Pa's voice brought her attention back to the trio outside the window. "Do you carry any ill will toward your uncle because of what happened?"

"I regret that whatever happened meant selling the ranch, but most of all I despise the secrecy. Better to know the truth and be able to deal with it." Walker shifted and looked straight at Josie. She didn't blink. But she felt his accusation like a sword piercing her soul.

He wanted honesty, but the only secret that bothered him was the longing to know why his uncle left. Seemingly a decent sort of man.

Not like *her* uncle. He was a cheat and a thief and taught her to be the same. By the time she realized that he sent her into a store to divert the owner's attention so he could steal something, she was in too deep to escape. When she tried to, her uncle pointed out that the sheriff would be happy to punish her for her part in the thefts. Not until she turned twelve, and Uncle's partners started making inappropriate comments about her, did he turn her over to the Kinsleys. Or it might have been because she had approached the local sheriff a couple of times trying to get up the courage to tell him she didn't want to be part of the stealing. Either way, she was glad of a chance to start over.

But apart from what Ma and Pa knew, no one was aware of everything she'd done. Nor would they ever be. Not if she hoped to hold her head up in public and earn a living as a seamstress.

She turned back to the kitchen and set supper to cook.

Sometimes secrets were necessary.

CHAPTER 3

*W*alker accompanied the preacher around the building project and listened to his plans to take in those who needed shelter.

"People like you," the man said. "And Mrs. Norwood and her children. My wife and I know the Lord has asked us to feed the hungry, tend the sick, and take in the stranger."

"'Inasmuch as ye have done it unto one of the least of these my brethren, ye have done it unto me.' Ma taught me that passage. I'm grateful I found your home."

"Your mother was a godly woman."

"She was. And she used every opportunity to impress God's truth upon me. She said she knew she wouldn't be around forever to guide me, so she was building a sure foundation for my faith."

The preacher took him inside and explained how he meant to lay out the various rooms. Mostly they talked about personal matters. Walker found it easy to tell the preacher about his family and his travels.

The afternoon soon passed, and at Miss Josie's call, they returned to the kitchen for supper.

Walker found he had a hearty appetite after going hungry the last five days. At the preacher's invitation, he took a second helping of the mashed potatoes, brown gravy, roast venison, and garden-fresh vegetables.

"It's an excellent meal." He directed his comment to Josie, knowing she had prepared the food. "It's been a long time since I enjoyed such fare."

"How come?" Donny asked. "Just 'cause you were losted?"

Walker waved away Mrs. Norwood's scolding. "I don't mind answering the boy." He turned to Donny. "At first, it was because my mama was sick and couldn't cook, so I did it. I'll be the first to say I have very few cooking skills, though I have learned some basics. Then I was traveling. Once I worked for a crew who had a good cook." He sighed, remembering, then shrugged. "Next crew I was on had a cook who managed to burn everything."

"Miss Josie don't burn stuff," Donny said.

"Doesn't," his mother corrected.

"Doesn't what?" The boy seemed genuinely confused.

"Doesn't burn things."

"That's what I said."

The adults grinned at each other. Walker shifted his gaze from Mrs. Norwood to the preacher and last, to Miss Josie. She grinned at the child and then, as if feeling his attention on her, slowly turned to him. Her smile flattened. She jerked to her feet. "I made dessert." She filled individual bowls at the cupboard and carried them to the table.

The preacher ate his rice pudding and pushed his bowl away. "I need to do some studying for my sermon."

"Sir," Walker said, "should I work on the building?"

Pastor Kinsley considered his question. "You've just suffered an injury and gone hungry for a few days. Wouldn't hurt you to rest. In fact, if my wife had been here, I doubt she would have let you be up and about at all today. So, take it easy." Satisfied, he included the others. "If anyone needs me, I'll be in the church." He paused behind his daughter and squeezed her shoulder. "Thank you for the nice meal."

"You're welcome, Pa."

He left the house. Through the window Walker watched him cross to the church. What was he supposed to do with himself? He wasn't much good at twiddling his thumbs, even if his head still hurt and he felt weaker than normal.

Little Blossom's head tipped toward the table.

Miss Josie noticed. "Stella, take her to bed. You go too. You look weary."

"I hate to leave you with all the work."

"I don't mind."

"I'll help," Walker said.

Two women stared at him. Donny's mouth fell open. He closed it. "But you're a cowboy."

Walker laughed. "Remember I told you I took care of my mama when she was ill? That included doing dishes." And a lot of other things that would likely surprise Donny and the ladies.

"You run along," Josie said to Mrs. Norwood. "I'll manage just fine."

23

"We'll manage just fine," Walker echoed and pushed to his feet.

Mrs. Norwood helped Blossom down from her chair.

"I'm going to help too," Donny called after her.

"Good idea," his mother said. She turned to Josie. "Do you mind watching him?"

"Of course not."

Donny sidled toward Walker. "I'll be with the cowboy."

Walker grinned at the boy. "He's going to help with the dishes."

Donny looked ready to argue then tucked in his chin. "I guess that's what cowboys do sometimes."

Mrs. Norwood and her little girl went down the hall. A door closed quietly. Before Miss Josie could speak the words of protest that Walker saw coming, he stacked the dessert bowls and carried them to the dishpan. "Donny, you can bring the spoons." He poured hot water into the basin and started washing dishes. "Donny, there's a towel for drying."

Miss Josie stared at Walker.

"Do you object to having help?" he asked.

"No, but I can't help wonder if— Never mind. Thanks for helping."

Walker wished she had finished what she was about to say. But he wouldn't prod, especially with the child there.

She scurried around, bringing the rest of the dirty dishes and then putting away things as Donny dried them. Soon the kitchen was tidy.

Donny looked about. "Now what're we going to do?"

Miss Josie held out her hand. "I'll take you down to the river to play."

"Any objections to me accompanying you?" Walker hoped she would find it impossible to refuse him. He had no desire to sit alone in the house.

"Of course, you're welcome to come too."

Walker ignored how stiff her words were and looked around for his hat. Remembered he didn't have one and brushed his hand over his hair instead.

Donny ran ahead of them as they left the house, leaving Walker and Miss Josie to walk side by side. They passed a well-tended garden, crossed a dusty street, and then a strip of green grass. They followed a path through some trees and stood on the bank of a river.

"If I had realized it was this close, I would have washed here," he said.

Donny squatted to look at a bug.

Walker and Josie drew to a halt to watch him. For a moment, neither of them spoke.

Walker broke the silence. "I told you about me, but I don't know anything about you and your family."

"What would you like to know?" She kept her attention on the boy.

"Your pa said this town is called Glory. How did it come to get such a name?"

She chuckled. Her eyes filled with amusement.

He tried unsuccessfully not to stare, surprised at how the change in her countenance made him want to know more about her.

"Pa thought Glory had been named after a heavenly theme."

"I take it it wasn't."

"Nope. Seems the first store owner would stand on his step and watch the sunset. He'd say, 'Glory, but that's a beautiful sight.'" She laughed, her gaze on him, waiting for his response.

He chuckled. "So, what did your father say when he learned the truth?"

"He said Glory was the perfect name and the perfect place." She shifted her attention past him. "He told you about our brother, Josh?"

Walker nodded. "I hope your family is able to locate him."

"What Pa didn't say is Josh is the only child born to them. The rest of us are adopted."

"Rest of you? How many are there?"

She grinned, obviously enjoying his interest. Donny moved along the edge of the water, and Walker and Josie followed.

"There are six of us adopted girls."

His eyes widened. Pleasure at her delighted laughter warmed his heart. It had been a long time since he'd enjoyed spending time in a young lady's company. "That would explain all the other chairs at the table."

"That, and Ma's habit of inviting others to join us for Sunday dinner." She pulled her mouth into a frown. "Mostly young cowboys."

"Such as me?"

"I guess."

"You don't look very happy about it."

"I don't mind them visiting. I just don't care to be courted."

"Seems I heard something to that effect before."

26

"You overheard me at the church." She watched Donny dragging a branch to the water's edge.

"So where are all these sisters?" Walker asked.

"Two of them stayed back in Ohio when we moved here. Three of them married cowboys since we arrived."

"Ouch."

She turned to him. "Why ouch?"

"I think it must be hard for you to see them marry cowboys, considering your opinion of that breed of man."

The skin around her eyes crinkled, and a smile teased her mouth. "Not at all. My sisters are very happy, and that's all that matters. Besides, every one of those cowboys had a home to give them."

"Home is very important to you then?"

"You could say that."

He waited, wanting her to go on. When she didn't, he prodded. "Does that mean you were homeless at one time?" That would explain it.

She took in a long, slow breath then faced him. "I joined the Kinsley family when I was twelve. Prior to that, I did not know if I would have a place to lay my head at night."

"No child should live with that sort of fear." He held her gaze, offering sympathy and understanding. "In a very small way I can appreciate what you went through. I lost my home when my uncle and Pa sold the ranch. I was angry at both of them for a long time."

"I can understand why you would be. Are you still?" Her gaze bored into his, seeking answers, wanting to understand.

"My ma told me carrying unforgiveness toward my

father was wrong. That I should honor him. She said I needed to forgive him. I realized she was right when I found myself being eaten away by anger and bitterness. One day I simply told him I forgave him for his part in the loss of the ranch."

"That must have been hard."

"My pride stood in the way, but once I'd said the words and meant them, I felt almost free."

"Are you going to tell your uncle the same thing?"

He jerked back, her words like a blow. "I'm only finding him because of my promise to Ma."

Her look searched deeply, probing into his thoughts. "I know forgiveness isn't always possible."

He wanted to deny her statement, but he had no idea what she was talking about. Was she suggesting he needed to forgive his uncle, or was it something she needed to forgive? However, there was one truth he knew without question. "There is nothing God doesn't forgive."

Her attention had returned to Donny. "I have no trouble believing in God's forgiveness."

"Human forgiveness is a different matter?"

"A much different matter, wouldn't you say?"

He thought of Dianne. "I courted a gal once. She had plans for us that didn't suit me. She said she wanted a man with ambition. One who wasn't afraid to do what was necessary to get ahead."

"Ouch."

He grinned. "Yeah, it hurt."

"Did you forgive her?"

They studied each other intently. Her question made him realize something, and he slowly smiled. "What I did was easier. I walked away." His smile flattened. "Avoiding her was somewhat harder, as I couldn't leave town with my mother ill and needing me. I suppose I should thank her for being the instrument of my learning a valuable lesson."

Josie cocked her head. "And that would be?"

"Avoid women whose prime interest in me is money and possessions."

She jerked away. Then chuckled. "I'd say you were safe enough in that regard."

It took him a moment to realize she referred to his penniless state, and he laughed. "You're right. Any woman who expresses an interest in me will have to be prepared to have nothing."

Seeing as it was clear that they would never be romantically interested in each other, he relaxed. It might be nice to have a friend for however much time he was here, without any complicated feelings getting in the way.

Donny headed toward them, his hands cupped around something. "Look what I found." He held out his hands for Walker and Josie to see.

A salamander.

Walker hid a grin at the difference in expression between Donny—who was thrilled with his find—and Miss Josie—who wore a look of horror.

JOSIE BACKED away from Donny and shuddered. "It's slimy." She didn't care for any sort of reptile. They were all in the same category as snakes.

Walker squatted before the boy. "He's a nice one."

"Can I take him back with us?" Donny asked.

Josie shuddered again.

Walker grinned at her before he turned to Donny. "You might be taking him away from his home. Do you want to do that?" He waited, as if giving the boy time to consider his choice.

Josie watched Walker. He was good with Donny. And no doubt, good for him too. Donny liked the attention of Josie's brothers-in-law, but he only saw them on Sunday, and only if they were able to journey to town for church.

"Maybe I should leave him so he can find his way home." Donny set the salamander on the ground. The reptile didn't move. "He's not going."

Walker stood, his hand on Donny's shoulder. "I think he's afraid we might follow him. Come on, let's leave him alone."

The pair backed away.

Donny looked up at Walker. "You think he'll be here tomorrow?"

"I wouldn't think so."

Donny shrugged and ran ahead of them.

Walker and Josie fell into step as they followed him. "If that critter has any sense, he sure won't be hanging about for a little boy to find him."

She laughed and turned to him as they shared the joke. His eyes flashed blue. She blinked and looked away. "We should get him home and into bed."

"Does he share the room with his mother and sister?"

"He does. He's very protective of them. I never have to remind him to slip in quietly. They've had quite an experience. My sister, Flora, and her husband, Kade, found them in the dead of winter in their little farm-house. No heat. No food. Stella barely alive. Little Blossom only a little better. Can you imagine the fears poor Donny endured?"

"I'm happy to say I can't imagine, though perhaps you can to a better degree."

Her feet slowed. "At least he had his mother and her love." As soon as she spoke the words, she wished she had kept them locked up inside.

But rather than demand an explanation, Walker smiled. "There's something about a mother's love to compel a boy to do all sorts of good and noble things."

Her insides eased with his words. "You're referring to your mother."

"I am." His smile was warm with memories.

"I don't recall my birth mother, but Ma Kinsley has given me free, unfettered love, and I consider myself most fortunate."

"How long have you been with the Kinsleys?"

"Seven years now. And I have to say they are the best seven years of my life."

"I guess that makes you nineteen."

"I guess it does."

Walker had drawn to a halt. "Let me get this straight. You don't remember your mother, so I'm assuming she died when you were very young. You came to the Kins-leys when you were twelve. Were you with your father in those intervening years?"

"My parents died within days of each other. Some sort of illness. I don't know what it was, as I was too young to remember."

"How old were you?"

She would normally object to his probing questions, but the knowledge that he too had lost his parents and had an uncle he didn't seem to care for had, in her mind, formed an invisible bond between them. One that he no doubt was unaware of. "I was five. About Donny's age."

"From what you said, I'll assume you didn't go to an orphanage."

"I might have been better off if I had, but no, my uncle took me. He didn't exactly take care of me, but he was my guardian."

They had stopped walking although she was aware of Donny playing nearby. Walker looked deep into her eyes. "It seems we both have uncles who disappointed us," she said.

"It seems so." His acknowledging look brushed a tender spot inside her.

From the way he smiled, she guessed he was aware of something tenuous between them formed by the knowledge they shared about their uncles.

They reached the house, and Donny slipped in quietly to go to the bedroom he shared with his mother and sister.

The setting sun slanted through the church windows, allowing Josie to see Pa kneeling at a bench inside the sanctuary. She stood still, taking in the scene, finding joy and strength in the life she'd been granted. "They taught me about God and His love. They showed it to me in every way. They gave me a home and security."

"You have been blessed." Walker's reverent tone touched her.

"Yes, I have."

"I have been too, to end up here when I did." He

touched the bruise on his head. "The scoundrel who robbed me expected me to die out there."

"Thankfully, you didn't."

"As your pa said, God had other plans."

She smiled at him. "Pa's a firm believer in seeing God's guidance in everything that comes our way."

"Even a penniless, homeless cowboy?"

Their looks went on for several seconds as she considered his question and how to answer it. "I'm quite certain that God has plans for you." She thought of a verse Ma had the girls memorize. "The Bible says, 'For I know the thoughts that I think toward you, saith the Lord, thoughts of peace, and not of evil, to give you an expected end.' Ma and Pa say God's thoughts are His plans."

"I like the idea of peace, but what does 'expected end' mean?"

They leaned against the unfinished building. It seemed neither of them was ready to end the evening.

"I think it would refer to all the good things God has promised. It's like He's saying, 'Trust Me. I want your best. Remember My promises.'"

"I like that. It reminds me of Ma's favorite verse. 'And we know that all things work together for good to them that love God, to them who are the called according to His purpose.'"

"They do go together, don't they?" When had she ever talked so freely about her faith to anyone outside her family? She felt as if she and Walker shared something unique. It made her look at him with new eyes. A penniless cowboy with a deep faith.

It was a nice feeling. But not one that could unsettle

her plans. She knew what she needed and wanted in life —the ability to provide for her own needs and to never feel she must depend on someone else.

She pushed away from the wall. "I must say good night."

"Good night."

She hurried inside and up the stairs to the room she'd once shared with three sisters. Now she was alone and, for the first time, was grateful for that fact, as she was restless and couldn't settle. As she frequently did when she didn't feel ready to go to bed, she sat on a chair next to the window and picked up her latest sewing project. She often sewed for her sisters and mother and occasionally for other ladies. Her projects were often done at cost or less because of the circumstances of the women she made a garment for. But she wanted to get some good paying customers. She was creating a dress for herself that had all sorts of special touches. She had talked to Mr. White at White's store. He had suggested she hang a small poster by the yard goods, offering her services as a seamstress. If anyone inquired, Josie wanted the person to see a garment she had made. Once it was finished, she would wear this dress to church and every special occasion there was.

She glanced out the window to the partially finished addition. She'd barely gotten used to the idea of more rooms, and now someone was sleeping there. Her thoughts went over the conversation she'd had with Walker.

The verse he'd mentioned had long been her nemesis. How could all things work together for her good? Life with her uncle especially. Yet, she couldn't deny that joining the Kinsley family was a blessing.

Content with her lot in life, she smiled as she pictured Walker and Donny with the salamander. And the things he'd said about the value of his mother's love.

She chuckled as she recalled his words about avoiding a woman who wanted only his financial position. She didn't fit that category, because she intended to provide for herself.

And there was absolutely no danger that any woman would pursue him for what he owned.

CHAPTER 4

*A*fter a hearty breakfast the next day—Walker wondered if he would ever fill the hunger of going without food for five days—he accompanied the preacher to the addition.

"I'd like to get this partition wall done as soon as possible," Preacher Kinsley said. "I feel an urgency to provide more rooms. But then maybe it's more important to finish the shingling before we get rain." As he talked, he lifted boards to the wall, and Walker nailed his ends into place.

Walker had studied the layout of the building. "Looks like you hope to gain four rooms."

"That's right. A service room where the ladies can do laundry in the wintertime and provide extra storage, and then three bedrooms that can accommodate three in each room. Nothing fancy, mind you. Just a shelter from the elements, warmth, and good food. Josie and my wife will see to the latter." The preacher paused. "That Josie is a good cook. She says she never gets tired of preparing food."

Walker tucked that little bit of information in with the rest of the things he'd learned about the young lady. Was her love of preparing food a result of not having enough? But had she said that, or was he assuming it went along with not knowing where she would spend the night?

By midmorning, he and the preacher had completed the partition, giving Walker a complete room. "This curtain is fine for now." He'd hang the door later.

"Good. Then let's finish the shingles."

Walker followed the man from the building into the bright sunshine. He blinked as he almost bumped into Josie, who was carrying a basket of garden produce. "Whoops. Wouldn't want to spill that basket. Are you the gardener?"

Her laugh echoed the sound of the birds in the nearby tree. "Right now, I'm the cook, gardener, wash lady, and everything else. Not that I mind. I find work very satisfying." She continued on to the house.

Her pa watched her. "Josie is a good worker. Maybe too good."

"Too good? Is that possible?"

"I fear it might be in her case. I get the feeling she is trying to pay a debt she doesn't owe."

Walker mused on that as he carried a bundle of shakes up the ladder. He knelt at one side of the roof, the preacher at the other, and they lay a row of shakes and tacked them in place. Walker could see it would take most of the day to finish one side of the roof. He glanced at the sky. No sign of rain. Hopefully the weather would hold until it was done.

Donny poked his head over the edge of the roof. "Aunt Josie said to tell you dinner is ready."

Walker glanced at the preacher to see how he'd react to the boy at the top of the ladder.

The man's expression went from worried to careful in a flash. "Donny, back down the ladder. Slowly. Didn't I tell you to stay off it?"

"Aunt Josie said to call you." The boy's chin took on a stubborn jut.

"Thank you, and I appreciate it. Next time call from the ground. Okay?"

Walker and the preacher made their way to the ladder. Donny scampered down, sending Walker's heart into a frantic race. "Preacher, I don't mind saying that was nerve-wracking."

"The boy needs to be kept busy, but I've failed to do it. And by the way, I'd be pleased if you'd call me Jacob."

"Done." Sure made it easier than calling him preacher all the time. He waited as the older man descended, then followed him, dusting off his too-short pants. If he had some money, he would find a store and buy some new clothes, but he didn't have a penny to his name. He was taller than Jacob, so it wouldn't do him any good to borrow clothes from the man. What difference did it make? He wasn't trying to impress anyone. He'd scrub his own clothes as soon as he could. It would be good to don them again.

He and Jacob washed in a basin of warm water outside the door then entered the kitchen where a dozen succulent scents greeted him. He'd been increasingly aware of them throughout the morning. A platter of fried pork and a bowl of spicy-smelling applesauce sat in the middle of the table. Josie carried a large bowl of mashed potatoes over then returned to the stove to fill a pitcher with brown gravy and pour fresh-from-the-garden peas into a serving dish.

Walker couldn't keep back his appreciation. "What a wonderful feast."

Josie chuckled. "Speaks a man who went five days without food. I expect most anything would look good."

"*Most anything* wouldn't look as good or smell as good as this." He looked toward Josie. "You are an excellent cook."

"Why, thank you. I enjoy cooking."

"I told him that," her pa said.

Walker met Josie's guarded look with a smile.

"I 'elp wif peas," little Blossom said.

Josie set down the dishes and bent to hug the girl. "You sure did. So did Donny and your mama. Thank you all."

Donny sighed dramatically. "I wanted to help shingle the roof, but Ma said she'd tie me to the bed if I went up there." He shot Walker and Jacob a look that plainly begged them not to tell his mother he had climbed the ladder.

Walker looked to Jacob, who gave a little shrug, and they let it pass.

They gathered around the table. Jacob said grace, and then the food was passed. This time Walker wasn't quite so hungry and could enjoy the food simply for the pleasure of how well it was cooked and seasoned. And then Josie brought out cookies and coffee.

Walker wanted to say again how good the food was, but he had done so several times and thought she might get annoyed if he kept mentioning it.

They were about to leave the table when someone pounded on the front door. "Preacher," a man called.

Jacob hurried down the hall to let in the man. "Zeke, what can I do for you? You look terrible. Come in. Josie," he called. "Pour the man coffee." Jacob led a man into the kitchen.

"Zeke Haynes, this is Walker Jones. He's visiting for a while."

Walker shook hands with Zeke, noting how his hand trembled.

Josie set a cup of coffee before him and a plate of cookies.

Zeke crushed his hat between his palms. "Preacher, what I got to say isn't for little ears."

Mrs. Norwood rose. "Come along, children. Blossom, it's time for your nap. Donny, I'll read you a story."

"Aw, Ma. I want to hear—" He stopped as his mother took his hand and led him out of the room.

The adults sat, waiting for Zeke to speak. He sucked in air. "I was on my way to town. I was passing the Boulter place when the boy—he's about twelve, I suppose—ran out to stop me. He was crying. Said his pa had been gored by a bull. I followed him to where his pa lay. He was in bad shape. I helped him into the house. Between his wife and me, we cleaned the wounds as best we could. But he's quite a mess. He asked I tell you and said would you come and pray over him?"

"I surely will." The preacher reached for his hat. "Josie, bring me my Bible. And some of the carbolic acid your ma uses on wounds."

She hurried down the hall and returned with a black Bible that the preacher tucked under his arm. She pulled a little metal box out of the cupboard. "Ma keeps supplies in here. Do you want me to go with you?"

Zeke shuddered. "It ain't pretty."

"I've helped Ma deal with all kinds of injuries," she said.

"It will be a miracle if he survives."

The preacher patted the older man's shoulder. "I believe I can manage on my own. I know a God who performs miracles." He looked at Josie and Walker. His gaze lingered on Walker. "I trust my daughter will be safe."

"Pa." Josie sounded as shocked as Walker felt.

Walker gave Jacob look for look. He was an honorable man. He wasn't going to take advantage of the preacher's absence to do anything he shouldn't. "Sir, if you don't trust me, I will be on my way." He pushed to his feet and headed for the door.

"Pa." Josie's voice was low, full of pleading and maybe something more. Maybe displeasure that her father had judged her.

"Walker, wait. You have to understand that I don't know you well enough to know if I can trust you. But I'm going to give you a chance. You're welcome to stay. And Mrs. Norwood will be here as well."

Walker paused, his hand on the doorknob. He didn't much care to stay someplace where he wasn't trusted, but the preacher was right. How were they to know if he was true and honest? He slowly turned and faced the room. "Sir, you will soon learn that I am a man of my word. My ma has raised me right, and I would never do anything to dishonor her memory."

Jacob nodded. "Then I will be on my way. Zeke, are you going back there?"

"If'n you don't mind, I think I'll do the business I came to town for." Zeke bid them good-bye and left by the front door.

Jacob made for the door. "I'll be back for supper." A few minutes later he had saddled his horse and rode away.

JOSIE COULD HARDLY THINK. Why had Pa said such a thing? Didn't he trust her? It wasn't like she was alone with Walker. That would have been unacceptable. Stella was here. Too bad Ma was away, but Mrs. Smith had just delivered her eighth baby and couldn't manage on her own.

And then to say he'd be back for supper. Usually he said he'd be back when he was sure the person he visited was doing okay.

Josie drew back her shoulders and faced Walker. "I am sorry for what Pa said. It isn't like him." She'd thought he trusted her completely. Perhaps he still remembered how she'd lived before they adopted her. Would that never stop haunting her?

"No, he was right to warn me. Not that he needed to,

but how was he to know that? This time yesterday he hadn't even met me."

"Thank you for being so understanding, though I admit I feel embarrassed."

"No need. I promise, you have nothing to fear from me." He reached for the doorknob. "Maybe I can get the rest of the roof shingled before he gets back." And with that, he left the house.

Josie drew in a deep breath. Walker was more than gracious after the way Pa treated him.

Stella slipped from the room. "I can't rest until I know what's going on."

Josie glanced past her.

"I made Donny stay in the room until I returned."

Knowing Donny would be straining to hear what she said, Josie drew Stella to the far side of the kitchen and in a few words relayed the story.

Stella shuddered. "The Boulters have three children. What will they do if their father doesn't make it?"

Josie hugged Stella. "The same as you. Keep going."

"I'm in danger of losing my farm if I don't soon get my strength back."

"Kade is seeing to your farm, so don't you worry."

Stella returned to the bedroom, and Donny rushed out.

"What happened? I wanna know."

"My pa has gone to see a man who was hurt."

"Hurt? How? What happened? How bad? Is he going to die?" Donny's bottom lip quivered.

Josie understood that he was thinking of his own loss. "Donny, I don't know. Pa will tell us when he returns."

"It ain't right for pas to die."

She sat and drew him close. "You know what my pa said when he left? He said God could perform miracles. He can make Mr. Boulter strong and well. We just have to ask Him. Shall we pray?"

Donny nodded.

Josie held his hands between hers. "God, we know You are good and loving. Please see fit to heal Mr. Boulter. In all things, we choose to trust You. Amen."

Donny looked up at her.

"Do you feel better?"

He nodded. "You should have prayed for my papa."

She rumpled his hair. "We have to trust God to do what is best." Hearing a sound at the door, she glanced up to see Walker standing there, watching.

"I came for a drink," he said and went to the pump to get water.

Donny sidled up to him. "Can I help you?"

Walker drank the water, set the cup down, and studied the boy.

Josie watched, wondering how he would satisfy this eager child. Or if he would dismiss him. Tell him to stay out of the way.

"Well…" Walker spoke slowly. "You can't go up the ladder. Your mama has forbidden it. But I see Mr. Kinsley has left lots of scraps of lumber on the ground. Now if a person was to gather them all up, I think that person might be able to make a little building of his own."

"Me?" Donny quivered with excitement. "I could? But I don't know how to build."

"Tell you what. You gather up the lumber bits and sort

them out, and when I'm done with the roof, I'll show you how to construct a building."

The boy was out the door in a flash.

Walker turned to Josie. "I hope your pa won't mind that I've given the scraps to him."

Josie managed a trembling smile. The way Walker had treated Donny elevated her opinion of him several notches. "I expect he wouldn't object."

Walker left.

Stella chuckled. "You look stunned. Did Walker surprise you? Could it be that you are learning that a man's good traits outweigh his lack of possessions?"

Josie shrugged. She tried and failed to laugh. "I care not for possessions beyond the necessities of life." Home and shelter. Food enough for the day. Everyone deserved that. And kindness such as Walker had shown to Donny. Josie's throat tightened. It was that childish eagerness to help and please that her uncle had taken advantage of. If he had directed it to good like Walker just did with Donny, things might have been so different. But her uncle only cared about getting things without putting in an effort to earn them honestly.

Stella studied her a moment longer. "Someday I hope you find that love is worth more than security."

"How can that be? Love won't keep you warm, fill your stomach, or protect you from the elements."

Stella pressed her palm to her chest. "It gives you the strength to work for those things. Josie, I would trade my home any day for the return of my husband."

"What about your children? Would you deprive them of what they need?"

"Of course not. But I know that together we would build a future for them."

Josie stared out the window where Donny scooted about picking up the bits and pieces of wood off the ground.

Stella sighed. "I'll go rest now."

"Have a good nap." Josie shifted her position so she could see the roof of the addition. However, Walker was working on the far slope and she couldn't see him.

Donny sat on the ground and stacked the bits of lumber.

She smiled. The boy might be without a father, but he had a loving mother and the protection of Josie's family. At some point, the Norwoods would return to their farm. She shuddered as she thought of how they'd almost died out there.

It seemed having a home still didn't mean a person was safe. Verses Ma had taught her along with the other girls filled her thoughts. *He shall cover thee with His feathers, and under His wings shalt thou trust. Thou shalt not be afraid for the terror by night.* She trusted God. Or at least she tried to. But she didn't think even trusting Him would enable her to live the way Stella talked of. She didn't think love would be enough to keep her warm at night.

Realizing how long she'd been idly staring out the window, she pulled out a bowl and mixed together ingredients for a cake. While it baked, she browned meat for a stew then covered it with water and set it to simmer. The cake was done, and she set it to cool then took up a basket, intending to head to the garden for vegetables to put into the stew.

A crash shattered the silence. She looked out the window. Donny wasn't where she'd last seen him. Her first thought was he had climbed the ladder, and it had fallen.

She raced for the door, not knowing what she would find.

CHAPTER 5

*W*alker stared at the ladder lying on the ground. He'd bumped it with a bundle of shakes. The shakes were scattered across the yard.

Donny looked up at him. "How you gonna get down?"

"I guess I'll have to stay here until someone puts the ladder back up."

"I will." Donny grunted as he tried to lift it. In a couple of seconds, he straightened. "It's too heavy for me."

Josie raced around the corner. She saw Donny by the ladder and grabbed him by the shoulders. "Are you okay?"

"Course."

"Were you trying to move the ladder? Climb it?" She ran her hand along the boy's arms. "You're sure you're not hurt?"

Donny moved out of her reach. "I'se fine. But Mr. Walker is stuck on the roof."

Josie looked at Walker.

He studied her, liking that she had to tip her head back to study him. "I bumped it."

Her eyes sparkled. Her lips quivered, and then she laughed.

Her humor was so unexpected he wasn't sure how to respond. "I'm stuck here." He tried to sound wounded, but his situation suddenly struck him as funny, and he chuckled.

She looked at the ladder than back to him. "It looks heavy. I don't know if I can lift it."

He hoped she was teasing. "I could get hungry and thirsty up here."

"I'll throw you a rope, and you can use it to draw up a bucket of water." Her expression revealed nothing.

He tried to guess if she was serious or not. Decided to play along with the game if that was what she intended. And if she didn't, he might as well settle in for a few hours on the roof. He looked around. "Nice view from up here. Your garden is very neat. Not a weed in sight."

"At least not from where you're sitting. However, if you were closer, you'd see some."

"I see people walking along the street."

"That would be Main Street."

He read the sign he could see. "White's Store."

"There's also a barber shop, Sylvie's diner, and the hotel. Across the street is the sheriff's office. Turn your head a bit and you'll see a big red barn. That's the livery barn."

"Do you suppose if I hollered real loud someone would come rescue me?"

"I don't know. Why don't you give it a try?"

Donny shuffled from one foot to the other and looked worried. "You're teasing him, aren't you?"

Josie laughed. "Yes, I am. Hang on Mr. Jones, and I'll see what I can do with this ladder."

He knew the ladder was heavy and held his breath as she struggled with it. She managed to get it against the roof, but it was at a precarious angle. He reached out to straighten it. His foot slipped.

"Stop." Her face paled. "Let me do it."

Having no wish to land in a heap at her feet—or anyone's feet for that matter—he sat back and let her straighten the ladder.

She shook it. "I think it's safe."

He backed down, reached the ground, and looked at her. "Thank you."

She nodded, her gaze dark. "You scared me."

"I'm sorry." He didn't move. He wanted her to know he hadn't meant to frighten her, any more than he meant to send the ladder to the ground.

"We don't need any more accidents around here, Mr. Jones." She spun around and headed for the house.

"Please call me Walker. Mr. Jones is my uncle." Walker smiled as he started to collect the shakes. Donny helped him. She was concerned about him. That was nice.

By rights, he should pay for the broken shingles, which meant he'd have to work for Jacob a few more days. Somehow, he didn't mind the idea.

Maybe he'd send a letter to Bella Creek and see if he could locate his uncle. That way he wouldn't have to spend any time looking for him.

He set aside the broken bits of wood and climbed back to the roof to continue the task.

A little later, he watched Josie make her way to the garden with a hoe. He couldn't see any weeds, but she obviously did, for she chopped away at the ground. She paused for a rest and looked his direction.

He smiled and touched the brim of his hat—except it wasn't there.

She nodded and returned to work, and he did the same.

Donny wandered away to join his mama and little sister when they emerged from nap time.

The afternoon passed. Walker's stomach growled. Wasn't it suppertime yet? But no one called him for the meal. He eyed the remaining part of the roof yet to shingle. Still a couple of hours work.

His stomach growled again, and he made his way to the edge of the roof so he could see down to the kitchen although he couldn't see inside. He sniffed. Sure smelled like supper.

Had they forgotten him?

He climbed down the ladder and went to the back door where he hesitated. Should he knock or walk right in?

He tapped lightly and stepped inside. The table was set. Mrs. Norwood sat with Blossom on her knee. Donny leaned against her chair.

Josie stood in front of the stove. "Pa isn't back," she said. "He said he would be back for supper."

Walker glanced at the clock over the cupboard. Seven o'clock. No wonder his stomach said it was suppertime. "The children must be hungry. Perhaps you should let them eat."

Donny nodded.

"I suppose that makes sense." Josie carried a pot of stew to the table and dished up some for the two little ones. "Stella, you should eat with them." She put stew on a third plate and stood there as if she didn't know what to do.

Stella got her children seated and took their hands. "I'll pray."

Walker closed his eyes, but as soon as the amen was said, he studied Josie. Her gaze went repeatedly to the hallway, as if she expected her father to come in the front door at any time. She turned and stared out the window by the back door. "He should have returned. It's not like him."

"Do you think he's run into trouble?" Walker asked.

"I don't know. Perhaps Mr. Boulter needed him. You know…" She trailed off without finishing, but he knew what she meant. Perhaps the man had succumbed to his injuries, and the preacher felt he needed to stay with the family.

"Would you feel better if I went and found out what's delaying him?"

Her breath whooshed out. "Would you?"

"Sure." He waited for her to suggest a way of getting there other than walking.

"How you gonna get there?" Donny asked. "You got no horse."

Josie blinked. "Go to the livery barn and ask for one. Tell Mickey the preacher needs it."

Walker reached for his hat, remembered he didn't have one, and left the house. He trotted over to the big red barn and introduced himself.

The tall, rangy man with a neat moustache and his

long blond hair tied back with a length of leather pointed toward a wagon and a pair of horses. "They're ready to go. Just came back from a short drive. Take them."

Walker would sooner ride a horse than drive a wagon, but the man seemed pleased that he could offer this, so he thanked him. "Can you give me directions to the Boulter place?"

"I heard about the accident. I hope he's okay." He waved his hands as he told Walker how to get there. "And Godspeed."

"Thanks." Walker was soon on his way from town, going west toward the Boulter place. He kept his attention on his surroundings. Perhaps the preacher's horse had come up lame. But he didn't see man or animal, and half an hour later, reached a set of buildings.

A half-grown boy greeted him. "Can I help you?"

"This the Boulter place?"

"Who wants to know?"

"Walker Jones. I'm staying with the Kinsleys. I came to see if the preacher needed anything. How's your pa?"

"Pa ain't as bad as we thought. Just that there was lots of blood and dirt on him. But the preacher ain't here. He left some time ago. You sure he ain't in town?"

"I guessed I missed him. Thanks for your help, and good to hear about your pa." Walker turned the wagon around and headed back down the road. He drove slowly, looking for clues on the road. Not satisfied with what he could see from his perch, he jumped down and led the horses, stopping every few yards to search the surrounding area. The road curved close to the river.

He stopped and studied the trees growing along the water. Maybe he should look there.

He pulled the horses after him, tying them to the nearest tree. He couldn't imagine why Jacob would be there, but he had to be sure. A broken branch indicated someone had passed by. He followed the narrow trail through the trees. The gurgle of running water informed him he had almost reached the river.

Knowing that there might be a reason for caution, he slowed and studied the view. A body lay on the grassy bank. It could be Jacob, though he couldn't be certain. He edged forward, searching for danger. He saw nothing to give him pause and rushed toward the man.

It was Jacob. A wound on his head oozed. His hair was matted with dried blood.

Walker turned him onto his back. "Jacob. Can you hear me?"

The preacher groaned and reached for his head.

"What happened?"

"I was robbed." Jacob tried to sit up but wobbled and fell back to the ground. "He took everything." He touched his head. "Even my hat. He wasn't satisfied with robbing me. He hit me with his pistol."

Same as what happened to Walker. "Did you notice anything about the man?"

"He had his face covered, but there was a cut on his hand. Like this." Jacob drew a line down the back of his hand along the thumb to the wrist.

"It sounds like the same man who robbed me."

"It pains me most that he has my Bible."

"Lay still and I'll clean you up." Walker went to the river and cupped water in his palms. Using his shirttail, he dabbed at the dried blood in Jacob's hair. "You have a good-sized goose egg." Walker watched the man as he worked. Several times he opened his eyes, and each time he hurriedly closed them, but Walker had seen that Jacob was having trouble focusing. "I'd say you're going to have a dilly of a headache for a bit."

"I'll be okay in a minute."

"Take your time." Walker studied the situation. He couldn't bring the wagon any closer, but he doubted Jacob could make it the distance to where it was tied. At least not on his own.

"I need to get home." Jacob again tried to sit but moaned and crumpled to the ground. He turned his head to the side and vomited.

Walker knew that wasn't a good sign. He had to get Jacob home as soon as possible. "You can't walk on your own, but I'm going to help you to your feet, and then we'll make it to the wagon on the other side of the trees."

He grabbed Jacob under the arms and leaned his entire weight into the lift. He managed to get Jacob upright, pulled one arm around his shoulders, and held it tight. He clamped his other arm around Jacob's waist and, together, they stumbled through the trees.

By the time they reached the wagon, they were both sweating and out of breath. Walker tipped Jacob over the end of the wagon and pushed him aboard.

Jacob groaned and curled up on his side.

"I'll get you home as quick as I can." Walker was headed for the wagon seat when something in the trees caught his eye. It looked like…

He trotted over and picked up Jacob's Bible. It was tied shut with leather straps, so even though it had been tossed aside, it was still intact. He took it to the wagon and put it in Jacob's hands.

Jacob mumbled, "Praise God."

Walker slowly guided the horses, knowing that every bump sent pain through Jacob's head. Back on the trail, he urged the horses into a trot.

He glanced back at Jacob several times. The preacher clutched the Bible to his chest. At least he was breathing. Walker prayed aloud, "Lord God, please let Jacob be okay." He repeated the words over and over until they reached town. He guided the wagon as close to the back door of the manse as he could.

Josie ran out. "Where is he?"

Walker pointed to the back of the wagon. She raced around and saw her father. "Oh Pa, what happened to you?"

Jacob moaned.

Walker answered her question. "Same thing as happened to me. Only my head is harder." He jumped down. "Help me get him into bed." He climbed into the wagon and eased Jacob to the end.

Together he and Josie half carried, half dragged Jacob inside and down the hall. She threw back the covers on a wide bed, and Jacob lay down.

Josie bent over to examine the wound. "Who did this?" She pulled off his boots and tossed them aside.

"He was robbed."

Josie wrung her hands. "I think I should send for Ma."

Jacob stirred himself enough to say, "No. I'll be fine. Just let me rest." The effort to speak left him breathless.

"Is there a doctor?" Walker asked.

"Not close by."

Jacob opened one eye and looked at Josie. "You know what to do."

Walker was certain the man had passed out. Was this injury going to kill him?

* * *

Josie wanted Ma. Yes, Ma had taught all of them how to tend the ill and injured. But this was Pa. And he was hurt bad. "I should take his clothes off. They're dirty." She couldn't bring herself to do so.

"Step outside while I remove them."

She gratefully ducked out the door and waited for Walker to call her back.

When he did, she returned to Pa's side. "I wish Ma was here."

Walker touched her arm. "He has faith in you."

"Despite what he said, I don't know what to do."

"If she was here, what would she do?" Walker's calm voice went a long way to settling her, and she sucked in air.

"She'd wash his wound. And keep him flat."

"Then that is what you must do."

"Right." Her hands trembling, she removed the pillow from under her father's head.

"I'll stay with him while you get water." He snagged a nearby chair and sat down.

Josie hurried from the room and quickly told Stella that Pa had a head injury.

"What happened?" Donny asked.

But her voice failed, and she couldn't answer. Thankfully, Stella drew him away. "He's been hurt. Aunt Josie is going to take care of him."

Josie filled a basin with warm water, gathered towels,

and returned to the room.

Donny followed, but his mother ignored his protest and led him away.

Walker rose and headed for the door.

"Please stay," Josie murmured. "I'm not feeling very brave." In fact, her limbs were ready to melt into a boneless puddle. Having Walker there, calm and encouraging, made it possible to keep functioning.

"Very well." He stood at the end of the bed.

Josie knelt at her pa's side. "Pa, I'm going to wash your wound. Okay? Pa?"

No response. Her heart stalled. She turned to Walker. "He's unconscious?"

He nodded. "It's a good time to deal with his injury. He won't feel it."

She held his gaze a moment, saw the depth of concern, and understood what he didn't need to say. This was not a good sign. But she must do what she must do.

She swallowed hard and gently cleaned Pa's hair. Done, she moved aside the basin and soiled towels and sat back on her heels, watching the rise and fall of Pa's chest, catching her breath every time there was a pause.

Walker moved the chair closer to the bed and guided her to it. "All you can do now is watch and wait and pray."

"I have no words." She looked at him. "Will you pray?"

He bowed his head. For a moment, he didn't speak, and then he began. "Lord God, as this man said, You are a God of miracles. We're asking You for one this evening. Please heal the preacher." His slow, deep-toned words filled the room even as it filled Josie's heart with courage and strength.

He touched her shoulder. "I have to return the horses and the wagon, but I will be back as soon as possible."

She barely heard him leave the room, but a shiver of fear crossed her shoulders when she realized she was alone with her injured father and helpless to do anything. But pray. She clung to the words Walker had uttered.

Sometime later she looked up as he returned.

He smiled…a steady, encouraging look. "Any change?"

"No." She continued to watch for Pa's chest to rise and fall.

Walker pulled a kitchen chair in with him and parked it beside her. "I reported the robbery to the sheriff. He's getting together a posse."

The words barely registered.

Time stood still as they kept vigil.

A sound outside the house distracted her.

Walker rose to see what it was. "You need to see this."

She shook her head. There was nothing more important than waiting for her Pa to open his eyes and recognize her.

Walker urged her to her feet, took her hand, and drew her to the window. The last of the daylight faded, but in the shadows at the front of the church, she made out a dozen or more people, some holding lanterns. "Why are they here?"

"I believe they have come to pray for your father." As he spoke, three more joined the group.

By the light of the lantern carried by the latest arrivals, Josie saw that they all stood with heads bowed. Her throat tightened. Ma might not be here, but she was not alone. She was surrounded by those who loved her pa and encouraged by the presence of a man she'd only recently met. She wondered at the confidence he provided for her, but rather than question it, she'd gladly accept it.

Strengthened and encouraged, she returned to her father's side.

Walker sat beside her. He said nothing. But having him there was all she needed from him.

Pa stirred and moaned.

She sprang forward. "Pa. Pa. Are you awake?" But he didn't respond.

Walker lit a lamp and put in on the table by the bed so they could see her pa.

Her head fell forward, and she jerked awake. She looked at Walker. He leaned back in his chair, but his eyes were wide open and watchful. "What time is it?" she asked.

"After midnight. Stella and the children are asleep."

"Are there still people out there?" She tipped her head toward the window.

"Last I looked, there were more than before."

"That's nice." She gathered her strength around her. "You don't need to stay here if you don't want to."

His blue gaze held her like a steady grip. "You shouldn't be alone."

"Thank you." She sat back, waiting and watching.

She drifted off again and jerked as her head dropped forward.

Walker touched her arm, drawing her attention to him. "I'll stay with him if you want to rest a bit."

"I can't leave him." She'd seen no change, and that worried her. A little later her head again fell forward, pulling her from sleep. Gray light filled the room. Walker reached out and turned down the lamp until the flame went out.

She went to the window. A crowd of people still gathered in front of the church. "Have they been there all night?"

"Some have. Others have left, and others took their place."

Stella poked her head in the door. "Any change?"

"I'm afraid not."

"We'll keep praying. Come along, children." She shepherded the children away.

A pot rattled on the stove, and Josie guessed Stella was preparing breakfast for the children.

A bit later, Stella returned with a tray. "Breakfast for you both."

"I didn't expect that." Not that Josie minded. The coffee smelled good and would revive her. Eating gave her something to do besides worry. "Thank you."

Walker and Josie shared the tray as they ate breakfast. Thankfully, he didn't seem to feel a need to talk.

The front door opened and shut. Josie assumed Stella was sending Donny out to play. Likely she was tired of dealing with the boy's questions.

"Oh."

The sound brought Josie's attention to the bedroom door. She sprang to her feet and ran into her mother's arms. "I'm so glad to see you. Pa wouldn't let me send for you." Thank goodness someone else had done it.

Her mother stroked Josie's hair. "I'm here now." She looked past Josie to her husband. "How long has he been unconscious?"

"Since last night. He's stirred a couple of times but nothing more."

Walker stood by the bed.

"And who is this young man?"

Before Josie could answer, Walker spoke. "Walker Jones, ma'am. I found your husband. He'd been robbed by the same man who robbed me." He touched his head to indicate he'd also been hit there.

"Thank you for your kindness," Ma said.

"I'm only returning the good deed. Your husband helped me after I was robbed." He stepped aside as Ma knelt at the bedside.

"Jacob, wake up. We need you."

No response.

Ma bowed her head into her palms, and her lips moved soundlessly.

Josie knew she prayed. She signaled to Walker, and they tiptoed from the room.

A wagon rattled into the yard. She looked out the window. "Flora and Kade." She rushed out and threw herself into Flora's arms. "God bless whoever thought to send for you."

"How is he?" Flora asked. Her red hair had been hastily braided as if they had left home in a hurry.

Kade patted Josie's back. "We need to be together at a time like this."

They barely made it to the house before another wagon approached.

"Eve and Cole. And they have Victoria and Reese with them." All three married sisters and their husbands were there. Josie was surrounded by those who loved her.

Walker stood by the door, and she introduced him.

"He brought Pa home," she said.

The men all clapped him on the back and thanked him.

"I'm certain Jacob was robbed by the same man who robbed me and left me with nothing. Took my horse, my tack, my supplies, and even my hat."

"What makes you think it was the same man?" Cole asked.

"The preacher was able to talk a bit when I found him. He said the man had a cut from the base of his thumb to his wrist. So did the man who took my things and then hit me over the head for no reason. Same as he did with Jacob."

"At least we'll be able to identify the man if we ever see him." Reese's words offered a bit of comfort.

"How's Pa?" Eve asked.

Josie gave them an update of their father's condition, then they went to the bedroom. Ma sat on a chair by the bed, and when she saw the family, she held out her arms to them. "I'm so glad to see you all." Everyone hugged her.

"He's going to be okay," she told them. "I feel it in my heart."

No one argued, and Josie hoped her mother was right.

Reese slipped out to inform those keeping vigil that Pa had not yet wakened. He returned a few minutes later. "They intend to stay until he is awake."

Josie bit her bottom lip. How long would it be before they knew what the outcome would be for Pa?

CHAPTER 6

*W*alker soon found himself standing with Josie's brothers-in-law as she and the girls took over the kitchen. He studied the others. Flora had a mane of red hair. Her husband, Kade, was tall and angular. Eve had black hair and blue eyes. Her husband, Cole, was a big man, head and shoulders above the others but with a gentle bearing. The third sister, Victoria was a fragile-looking blond married to Reese, a man with black hair and black eyes who watched her constantly with an adoring look.

The ladies made coffee and cookies and took them out to the people waiting and praying at the church.

The three men wanted to tour the addition, and they made comments about the work. They worried how the preacher would get around without a horse.

"Sure hope Ma is right about him getting better." Reese no doubt spoke for all of them.

Walker saw the pile of wood that Donny had collected. The boy followed them around. "I haven't forgotten that I promised to help you," Walker assured him.

The others wanted to know what he had promised.

"I told Donny if he collected the scraps of wood, I'd help him build something."

"Let's all do it," Cole said.

So, the men sat on the ground by Donny's pile of lumber.

"What did you have in mind?"

"A barn," Donny said. "I keep the one Pa made me inside, so it won't get ruined." His bottom lip trembled, and the men quickly picked up pieces of lumber and examined them.

Donny's attention shifted to the project.

With plenty of good-natured joshing about who had the best idea, the men guided Donny in the construction of a barn. It wasn't yet finished when the ladies returned from serving coffee and joined them.

The discussion turned to how they would take turns staying with their father until he was better.

"We'll have to make sure Ma gets some rest," Eve said. "You know she'll balk at the idea."

"We're prepared to stay overnight and as long as is necessary," Flora said with some degree of heat.

"So, let's sort out how we'll do it." Eve seemed the most logical of the ladies.

They decided that each couple would take turns sitting with Jacob while their ma rested. "We'll have to promise to waken her if there is any change."

"I'll take a turn," Josie said.

"You shouldn't be alone. It's too difficult to stay awake."

Walker spoke before he could think how they'd react. "I'll sit with Josie. I owe the preacher that much." He'd explained how Jacob had taken him in and offered him employment until the addition was finished.

Every pair of eyes turned to him. Stared and then shifted to Josie and stared.

Walker had no idea what was going through each mind. Though he suspected they were seeing things that didn't exist. "As you said, Josie shouldn't be alone. I'm the most logical one to stay with her."

"Logical, is it?" Flora said, her green eyes bright. "About as logical as getting stranded in a snowstorm."

Kade pulled her close. "Not everything is logical," he said.

Walker must have looked as confused as he felt, for the others laughed, and in a burst of words explained how Flora had been out riding…

"Against Pa's wishes."

And had gotten lost in a snowstorm…

"I believe it was God's hand that led me to Kade's home." Flora looked as pleased as a bee in a lush patch of flowers.

"So, Pa insisted they must marry."

The others laughed, but Flora scowled. "Nobody could make me marry."

"And yet you are married." Eve spoke gently.

"Because Kade made me love him. So, I married him because I wanted to."

Kade hugged her. "It was easy to make you fall in love with me. I think you did so right from the first but were too proud to admit it."

Victoria had been mostly silent until now. "Flora

knows what's she's doing. She doesn't intend to let Kade think he has her in the palm of his hand."

Reese leaned back and studied his wife. "What are you saying?"

She gave him a smile so sweet that Walker imagined she could have asked Reese for anything at that moment. "I'm just saying all of you need to understand that we married you because we love you."

Walker turned away from the obvious affection between them. They seemed so certain of their love for each other. Would it survive disappointments and changes?

The ladies went inside to prepare dinner. After they'd eaten, Eve and Cole sat with Jacob while the other ladies insisted their mother go upstairs and rest, promising they would call if there was any change whatsoever.

Walker looked at the half-finished building. He had only a little bit of the roof left to shingle, but he was afraid the sound of hammering might bother Jacob, so he went to the little barn Donny was constructing. Kade and Reese joined him, and they soon had it finished.

The afternoon passed slowly. It seemed no one wanted to do anything until the preacher returned to his senses. People still congregated in front of the church, coming and going according to what their responsibilities required.

Several times someone would come to the house and ask after the preacher.

Then an old cowboy sauntered over to them. The girls were instantly on their feet. "Mr. Bates, it's so good to see you." The men rose and shook hands with the man. Reese introduced Walker to the older man. "This cowboy has been a faithful friend to the whole family. He's even preached a few fine sermons when the need arose."

Mr. Bates made a dismissive sound.

Reese continued. "Walker has been helping Pa with the construction. He found Pa when he was missing and brought him home."

"Good man."

Walker couldn't explain why it should be, but the man's two words of praise were like a blessing.

Mr. Bates turned back to the ladies. "I came as soon as I heard. How is your pa?"

"No change,"

"May I see him? I'd like to pray for him."

Josie led Mr. Bates inside.

"It's so good to see him," Victoria said. "I feel like things will be okay now that he's here."

Eve and Cole joined them. "Ma is in there with Mr. Bates."

The ladies turned their attention to supper, and soon they were crowded around the table, with Mr. Bates joining them. They kept their voices low as they visited.

Victoria and Reese went to the bedroom, and Josie brought Ma out.

Bedtime approached. "The girls will sleep upstairs," Eve said. "Just like old times."

"The men can bed down in the addition," Ma said.

Cole led the way. "Wake us up when it's our turn to sit with Pa."

"One of you can have the cot." Walker couldn't imagine taking the cot while the others spread bedrolls on the floor. Of course, he didn't have a bedroll, which Kade pointed out.

So, he reluctantly took the only bed, and the others stretched out on the floor as darkness descended.

"The girls will be enjoying their time together," Kade said.

Walker listened to the men talk. They seemed so happy. But he knew how quickly that could end. He'd once known a happy home…until Uncle Paul left. Things changed after that. Pa's shoulders grew bowed, and he was short tempered. Ma grew quiet and serious. Even in the last year of her life, as she grew weaker with each passing day, and, although her faith was strong, it seemed something had gone from her spirit.

The men turned their talk to cows and ranching. Walker tried to listen, but he hadn't slept the night before and couldn't stay awake.

His last thought was that these men had land and homes to offer their wives, and he was only a penniless, homeless cowboy.

* * *

Victoria shook Josie awake. "Your turn," she whispered.

They both moved as quietly as they could so as not to disturb Ma, who shared Josie's bed, but despite their caution, Ma sat up. "Is he awake?"

"No, Ma." Victoria rubbed her mother's back. "Lie down again. We will let you know if there is any change."

Ma looked ready to argue then sighed. "Very well. I know you girls are every bit as capable as I am." She settled back on the bed.

Josie pulled her dress on and tiptoed downstairs.

Gray light filled the windows and pooled on the floor. She glanced toward the church. Only a few people remained, most of them sitting on the steps or the ground.

Mr. Bates had unrolled his bedding in the addition, but through the kitchen window she glimpsed him sitting on the ground outside, his back to the wall, his head tipped down. She couldn't tell if he slept or prayed.

She slipped into Pa's room and studied him. His color was good. "Pa," she whispered. There was no response. She sat at the bedside.

Reese had been with Victoria. He was to waken Walker and send him to keep Josie company. She wondered if he would choose to stay in bed. Not that she would blame him. He wasn't part of the family and had no reason to inconvenience himself.

But her heart lightened as he stepped into the room. It was nice to have someone to keep vigil with her. Made it less frightening and the time would pass more quickly.

"How is he?" Walker asked.

"No change."

He sat beside her. "How are you?"

She stared at him, surprised that he asked. Everyone simply expected her to do what needed to be done. And she expected the same of the others. To have him voice concern jarred her. But it also pleased her to a degree. "I'm fine. All that matters is how Pa is doing."

"It matters a lot, but I think you matter too."

She couldn't stop staring. His gaze held hers. She jerked her attention back to her pa and put up mental barriers against the way Walker's words had touched her. She would not allow silly dreams into her life. She had secrets she couldn't share. Secrets that meant she kept others at a safe distance.

They sat in silence for some time until Walker broke it.

"I keep thinking we should do something."

"Like pray?"

"That of course, and I have been, as have dozens of others. But what if he can hear us? What would he want to hear? Perhaps hearing something would help him come back."

It was an interesting thought. "It's worth a try. Two things he'd like to hear—singing and Bible reading."

Walker grinned. "I heard you sing in the church. Why not sing for him?"

Josie felt embarrassed to sing with an audience of two, but her love for her pa made her dismiss the feeling. She would sing for an audience of one—Pa.

Keeping her voice low so she wouldn't disturb those still sleeping, she sang the song Walker had overheard in the church. "Amazing grace, how sweet the sound."

She was almost certain that Pa turned toward her, and she sang the song over.

Pa's Bible was on the table by the bed. She handed it to Walker. "Your turn. Read to him."

He opened the pages and read the Twenty-third Psalm. It was one of Pa's favorites, and Walker's strong, clear voice filled the words with hope and faith.

The children's voices in the hallway informed everyone that it was morning.

Stella came to the door to inquire after Pa.

Josie was about to say, "No change," when she noticed Pa's eyelids flicker. She caught her breath and waited, hoping and praying he would wake up. But he released a sigh and lay still.

Eve and Flora tiptoed into the room.

Josie caught their hands on either side. "I think he likes hearing us sing. Join me." They stood side by side and sang several hymns in harmony.

"His eyes flickered," Eve said.

"I'll get Ma." Flora dashed up the stairs.

"I'm going to let Cole know." Eve hurried out the back door.

Josie fell to her knees by the bed. "Pa, can you hear me? Pa, wake up."

Walker's hand rested on her shoulder, and she grabbed his fingers and held on tight, drawing comfort and courage from his presence and his touch.

Ma burst into the room, with Josie's sisters on her heels. Josie left the bedside and joined the other girls. The brothers-in-law pushed into the room. Each reached for his wife and held her close, leaving Josie alone.

Walker moved to her side. He didn't touch her. She didn't reach for his hand. Instead she gripped hers together. But it was nice that he was there.

"Jacob, my love, wake up," Ma pleaded.

Pa cracked one eye open. "My head hurts." His voice was low and raspy, but he was awake.

Josie wiped away tears, and she wasn't the only one.

Ma held a cup of water to Pa's lips. "Praise God, you are awake."

Josie ran to the back door. "Mr. Bates, Pa is awake."

She ran through the house to the front door. "Everyone, Pa opened his eyes. He's awake." She wanted to shout it to the heavens. She laughed and spun around, right into Walker, who had followed her. Without think-ing, she hugged him. "He's awake." She laughed and cried at the same time.

Shouts of "Praise God," came from the church along with a cacophony of laughing and sobbing.

Walker's arms came around Josie's shoulders, and his eyes shone with joy. "He is indeed awake."

She looked up at him. It was wrong to be so intimate with a man she hardly knew, but it felt so right given the joy of the moment.

She smiled and stepped back. "It's a miracle."

Walker's arms returned to his side. "He said he believed in miracles."

They smiled at each other, the others forgotten until Donny ran up to them. "He's okay?"

Walker swung the boy into the air. "He's opened his eyes and talked."

Josie heard what he didn't say. That time alone would tell if he would come back to normal.

It was a happy crew that gathered around the table for breakfast, talking and laughing as they again and again told how Pa had responded to their singing.

Victoria finally crossed her arms. "I wish I'd been there. I would have liked to sing for him and see his eyes open."

"We'll get lots of chances to sing for him in the days ahead," Josie said. "In fact, we're done eating. Let's go sing for him now." She waved her hand to indicate the men. "You come too."

Walker looked uncertain. "You too," she said. "You're a big part of his being with us." Her throat closed off, and she swiped at tears. It was true. Not only had he found Pa and brought him home, but he had suggested singing and reading to him.

"This looks to be a family moment."

Josie looked around the circle of sisters and their husbands. "What do you all say?"

"You must come." They were all in agreement, so the eight of them crowded into the bedroom.

It was Eve who suggested a song. They sang "Rock of Ages." The men's deep voices ran along the bottom of the sound.

Josie smiled at Walker, and he joined them. His voice was rough, but it added an interesting sound.

Pa smiled the whole time they sang and sighed when they finished. "It was singing that drew me back. At first, I thought I was in heaven, then I heard someone read Psalm twenty-three."

"That was Walker," Josie said.

"Thank you for reading and even more for finding me and bringing me home." Pa's voice was weak.

"He's tired." Ma shooed them from the room. She paused at the doorway. "Is Jonathan still here?"

Mr. Bates stood at the kitchen door. "I'm here."

"Would you be so kind as to deliver a message at church tomorrow?"

"'Twould be my honor, though as you all know, I am not a preacher."

"Thank you. You're exactly what we need at the moment." Ma returned to Pa's side, and the others went to the kitchen.

"I plum forgot it was Saturday," Josie said.

"We'll have to prepare the Sunday meal." Eve looked about the kitchen. "This is just like old times."

"How many of you are staying?" Josie hoped she didn't sound as if their departure would be disastrous, but she surely would miss them.

All three of them assured her that they planned to stay for church.

The women turned to planning meals, and the men went outside. Josie heard them say something about looking after the horses.

She looked out the window, glad to see Walker walked with them.

Flora sidled up to her. "He fits right in, doesn't he?"

"Does he? I hadn't noticed." She went to the cupboard and pulled out a bowl to make a cake pudding for tomorrow. But she *had* noticed. The trouble was, he wasn't staying, and even if he was, it wouldn't be because of her… for three reasons.

First, he'd overheard her say she would never marry a penniless, homeless cowboy. And she meant it. She'd promised herself she would never again be dependent on a man who couldn't provide her needs. She'd be responsible for her own food and shelter.

Secondly, he planned on heading north, wandering about the vast western territory of Canada.

But the third reason was the most important of all. She must forever hide her past. If people knew the truth… She couldn't let herself consider what would happen. Even her family would look at her differently.

CHAPTER 7

*W*alker considered returning to the roof to finish shingling, but he feared Jacob's head might object to the noise, so he followed the men to the little barn at the back of the yard. They leaned against the top rail of the fence and talked as they looked at the horses grazing placidly.

"The preacher is without a horse," Reese said.

"Flora's been working on a couple." Kade mused a moment. "One of them might be ready. I'll ride out and get it."

Walker perked up at that. It seemed Flora was a horse trainer. Interesting young women these were. So warm and caring except he'd noticed the way Josie pulled back into herself from time to time and wondered if she had a secret she kept from the others.

He did not like secrets. One had destroyed his peaceful family. To this day, he wondered what it could be.

"I don't think there's a rush," Cole said. "No doubt

Flora will want to check on her pa in a few days. Let her bring the horse."

Kade chuckled. "She'd likely skin me alive if I did otherwise. So, it's settled?"

"We should know by tomorrow if the preacher is going to be able to manage on his own," Reese said.

"He won't have to." Walker straightened and faced the others. "I'm here. I'll make sure he's taken care of."

The three men studied him.

"Sounds fine to me," Kade said.

"Good." Walker shook hands with each of them.

"Let's wander through town," Cole said. "Reese here might want to check on some of his friends."

The three of them told him how Reese had recognized Victoria as a missing daughter of a rich man and had taken a job in town so he could watch her.

"I wondered if she was playing a trick."

"I take it she wasn't."

"No. She had amnesia. She still does. She reconnected with her family but didn't stay with them. Said it was like living with strangers."

Kade slapped Reese on the back. "Seems she preferred this old cowboy."

They reached Main Street, which Walker had seen from the rooftop. Every few feet they were stopped by concerned people and gave a report on the preacher's improvement.

Walker paused as they reached White's Store. "I need to take care of a few things. The rest of you go on without me." He stepped into the store while the others stood outside, talking to well-wishers.

The first thing Walker meant to do was buy some

new clothes if he could buy them on credit. He approached the counter.

"Howdy, stranger. You'd be the young man who brought the preacher in. I'm Norm White, owner of this establishment. Call me Norm. Pleased to make your acquaintance." Norm stuck out his hand and shook Walker's enthusiastically.

Walker could see that there were no secrets in Glory, and news traveled fast.

"What can I do for you?" Norm asked, his gaze searching Walker, measuring him. He must have been satisfied, for he leaned back and waited for Walker to answer.

"I need clothes, but I have no money."

"Not a problem. It's on the house for your part in rescuing the preacher."

Walker protested, but to no avail. In the end he stood before a pile of things—new shirt, new pants, socks, and even a new hat.

"If I could borrow a pencil and some paper, I need to write a letter."

Norm provided everything he needed.

Walker printed a letter to his uncle, informing him of his whereabouts and asking for directions to where he lived. *My mother asked that I speak to you.* There wasn't much else to say to the man who had ridden out of his life without explanation and left Walker's family badly bruised.

He pasted the letter shut. If Uncle Paul was in the vicinity of Bella Creek, he should receive the message. Otherwise... Walker knew he would have to keep looking in order to keep his promise to his ma.

Norm glued on a stamp.

Walker stepped outside, the brown-paper-wrapped bundle under his arm. The others were still standing in front of the store speaking to those who hurried over to ask them about the preacher.

Cole turned at his approach. "Good news. The sheriff has apprehended a man who fits the description you gave. Let's go on over to the jail, and if you identify him...well." Cole shrugged. They all knew the penalty for a horse thief.

They crossed to the jail. Walker recognized the man and told the sheriff about the scar on the back of his hand.

"That's good enough for me." The sheriff had him sign a statement, then Walker stepped back into the sunlight with a sigh of relief.

The others waited outside.

A young boy of about ten raced toward them.

"Reese, it's you. Ain't seen you in a long time."

"Almost two weeks, isn't it? Yup. Guess that's a long time." Reese introduced Jimmy. "He helped me when I was working in town."

Jimmy's chest expanded visibly. "Now I work at the livery stable for Mickey. He says I don't have to call him Pa even though he married my ma."

They stopped at Sylvie's diner, and a robust woman hurried out to greet them.

Walker thought she seemed especially fond of Reese, although she talked like the man was a royal nuisance.

They visited the livery stable.

Walker glanced toward the church. Or more correctly, toward the manse, wanting to return and assure himself all was well. He must have glanced too often, because Kade patted Walker's back and chuckled. "Anxious to get back and check on that little gal?"

"I was wondering about Jacob."

The others chuckled. "Of course, that's all there is to it." But they headed back to the church.

The girls and their husbands insisted their ma rest after supper and took turns staying with their father for several hours. But Mrs. Kinsley chased them away as it drew near bedtime.

"I'm going to sleep beside him. I'll know if he needs anything."

Jacob smiled. "You're all I need."

At that the others left the room so the older couple could be alone.

The married couples drifted off in pairs. Walker imagined they wanted time to talk about things in private. Stella had taken her children to bed. He didn't know where Josie had gone, but she was nowhere to be seen.

"Come and keep me company." Mr. Bates waved Walker over.

Glad of something to do, Walker sat beside the man, his back to the rough wood of the addition.

"You remind me of myself," the older man began.

"You were a homeless cowboy?"

Bates's laugh was deep and full. "Maybe so, but that isn't what I meant. You see, I was a man running from my memories."

"How is that like me?"

Bates looked toward the horizon. "I recognize in you what I had."

"I'm afraid I don't understand."

"Well, sir. I don't know the partic'lars of your situation. In my case, it was an unfaithful woman."

Walker forced himself to remain motionless. Bates couldn't know about Dianne. It was simply that, all too often, a woman proved to be unfaithful. "You are correct in thinking I was hurt by a woman, but I got over it. Time heals all wounds." Though some more quickly than others.

Bates continued. "I blamed the woman in my life for the path I chose. One that took me into a shameful way of life. Thank God, He found me and lifted me from the pit. But I carried a bucket of bitterness around long after God saved me. Bitterness toward that woman. Until I learned that the bitterness was destroying me and not hurting her a bit. So, I forgave her. Even if she doesn't know it. Or likely even care."

Walker nodded. "I had bitterness toward my pa for something he did." Though, thanks to the long-standing secret, Walker had no idea if Pa had done something or Uncle Paul had. All he knew was their family had been torn apart and wounded. "But my ma taught me I had to let it go, and I did."

Bates patted Walker's hands where they rested on his drawn-up knees. "Son, I'm mighty glad to hear that. But I don't think that's the end of it."

"How so? You think God demands more of me?"

"Son don't think me forward, but I've been sitting here nigh onto three hours except for a time to eat supper. And I've been praying. Mostly for Jacob in there. But God kept bringing you to my mind. I don't know what you need to do or who you need to forgive, but I'm convinced there is someone." He shifted to study Walker. "I think you know in your heart." Bates patted his own chest. "Who I mean."

Only one name came to Walker's mind. Uncle Paul. But he didn't know if there was anything to forgive, because he didn't know why his uncle had left. But… "I guess I've been disappointed with my uncle for leaving our ranch and making it necessary to sell it."

"Let it go, son. Let it go. It's the kind of thing that grows bigger with time."

Walker leaned back. "It no longer matters to me, so it's no problem to let it go."

Bates didn't say anything. He just leaned back beside Walker. "I pray God will show you if you need to do more."

They sat there, silent but not uncomfortable

Bates spoke again, his words slow and soft. "Son, what are your plans for the future?"

"I promised my ma I would find my uncle and let him know my parents have passed on. After that…. Well, I thought I'd keep riding north. Work some. Someday, maybe get my own place." He knew it sounded weak and rudderless.

"So, no real plans or goals. Why is that? Could it be that something is keeping you from wanting to settle down?"

Walker opened his mouth, intending to say he had lots of time to plan for the future, but Bates's words struck a tender spot in his heart. "Seems to me a man can't count on having something that lasts."

Bates made a sound that could be agreement or disagreement. "Things of this earth can be snatched away. They can disappear for one reason or the other. That doesn't mean a man is wrong to build a home while trusting God for the future. What does the Good Book say? 'God is our refuge and strength, a very present help in trouble. Therefore, will not we fear, though the earth be removed, and though the mountains be carried into the midst of the sea; Though the waters thereof roar and be troubled, though the mountains shake with the swelling thereof.' Ah such a sweet reminder that God is the One who holds our future safe."

They fell into another long, thoughtful silence until the others returned, then made their way to bed.

Walker wondered what Bates would say at the Sunday service. He was a simple-speaking man, but his words carried the wisdom of his years.

* * *

SUNDAY MORNING WALKER trotted to the river and scrubbed himself clean in the water. He donned his new clothes and went into the house to join the others for breakfast.

"Woo-eee," Bates said as Walker sat at the table. "You clean up real nice."

Walker's cheeks burned. He hoped he was brown enough from the sun that no one noticed. He would not look toward Josie to see her reaction, even when her sisters chuckled.

Cole sat on one side of him and tipped his elbow into Walker's ribs.

Donny sat on Walker's other side. "I think you look

good." He spoke heatedly, as if understanding Walker's discomfort.

Walker felt people staring at him but kept his attention on his plate hoping someone would soon say grace and pass the food. Just when he thought he wouldn't be able to endure the strain another moment, someone gasped. He jerked up to see what was wrong and saw Jacob and Mrs. Kinsley in the doorway.

"Pa, you're okay? You sure you should be up?" Four girls spoke at once.

Mrs. Kinsley waved away their concern. "Your father intends to go to church and thank all those who prayed for him." She led him to the head of the table, and he sat down gingerly.

"Shall we pray?" His voice was uneven, and it broke as he thanked God for the food and for his health. "Amen."

Walker joined the others in a heartfelt, "Amen."

"Do you want to deliver the sermon?" Bates asked.

"I don't think I'm up to that." Jacob's voice lacked its usual strength. "I'd appreciate if you took my place."

"My pleasure."

Breakfast was soon over, and the entire household crossed to the church. Mrs. Kinsley wanted to get her husband seated before the others began to arrive.

"I'll play the piano," Victoria said. "The rest of you can help with the singing."

They filed into two pews. Mr. and Mrs. Kinsley, Mr. Bates, Stella, and her children in the front one. Man and wife, man and wife, man and wife in the second. Then Josie slid in. Walker hesitated. There was room on either bench.

Josie looked up at him then down at the spot beside

her. Did she mean to invite him to sit with her? Next to her was Reese. He leaned closer. "Sit down and relax."

He did. The church began to fill with people. As soon as they saw the preacher sitting at the front, they made their way forward to speak to him, one by one or in family groups. Many dashed away tears.

Josie leaned closer, her whisper hidden by the sound of the piano and the low conversation in the pew ahead of them. "I didn't realize how beloved my father is."

"He's a good, kind man."

Her smile was shaky.

He resisted an urge to squeeze her hands and assure her that her father was going to be okay. Instead, he looked deep into her brown eyes and smiled.

Their gazes ended quickly, but he felt that she had let him see more of her than usual, and he sat back, rather pleased with himself.

Bates stood at the pulpit, and the congregation quieted to hear him. "I'm not a singer, so I'll stand here and sing the words to myself while the Kinsley girls help us." Josie and her sisters slipped out of the pew and stood by the piano to sing.

Walker knew he too was no singer, but he sure didn't mind listening to their sweet voices. And if his gaze sought Josie almost exclusively, no one would know. Except perhaps Josie, whose gaze flickered away from his and then returned. And maybe Eve, who nudged her, whereupon Josie kept her attention on the front of the church.

Walker smiled. He enjoyed the music. Partly it was. But a bigger part of his enjoyment was seeing Josie's reaction to him.

He lowered his head and forced his thoughts back to sensible. He was a penniless cowboy who had no plans to settle down in the near future. Josie would never see him as anything but a young man who needed the hospitality of the Kinsley home until he got his feet under him.

The girls sat down.

And he forgot all his talk about being a homeless cowboy as his senses filled with her nearness.

Bates cleared his throat then began to speak. "I'm a poor preacher. Fact is, I'm no preacher a'tall. But Jacob Kinsley asked me to say a few words, and I can do that." He paused and looked across the congregation. Walker wondered if his gaze lingered on him a moment longer than anywhere else.

Then Bates smiled and, speaking so softly that people leaned forward to catch every word, he began. "This week we have seen that God can do powerful things, haven't we? It makes me ask you all, is there anything too hard for God?"

Heads shook in silent answer.

"But sometimes we hold things back from God's power. Sometimes we want to cling to them. Things like unforgiveness and bitterness. Like blame and shame. And sometimes we don't think God can fix them. Like an uncertain future, failing health, the pain of loss. Folks, I'm here to tell you, there isn't anything God can't help you with if you let Him."

Walker was mesmerized by the words. He knew God could do anything. But he had been drifting through life since his ma died. Rudderless, homeless, without direction or purpose. Find his uncle and then what? He had no plan.

Why was that? What was holding him back?

* * *

Josie looked around the table where the family gathered for Sunday dinner. They hadn't invited any extras, though Walker and Mr. Bates were there. Her sisters had informed her that they would leave after the meal. She missed them already but understood they needed to get back to their own homes.

Ma kept a close eye on Pa. He was tired from the morning at church, and as soon as he stopped eating, Ma hurried him to bed.

The others finished soon after. The girls insisted on helping clean the kitchen before they left. And then there was a flurry of good-byes.

Stella and the children went to their room. Stella had told Josie that she was taking the children to visit a friend in town as soon as Blossom had her nap. She insisted Donny stay in the room with them so he wouldn't make a noise and disturb Pa. He had the barn his pa made him and the animals for it in the room so he could play quietly.

Josie looked around. The house was silent, and with no wish to disturb the peace, she slipped outside.

Walker leaned against the wall. "Everyone has gone."

"Yes."

"It will seem quiet without the others."

By silent agreement they walked toward the river.

"I will miss them, but I like being back to a routine. I like work."

"Your pa said you were trying to pay a debt you didn't owe."

She stopped and stared at Walker. "He said that? I don't know what he meant."

"I don't either, and I didn't ask, seeing as it's none of my business."

She shook her head, and they continued on their way, passing through the trees to the river. Pa's words tangled through her thoughts. "He knows I don't ever want to have to live like I was when they adopted me." She hoped he wouldn't ask her to explain how that was and hurried on. "I know I owe them, but that isn't why I like work. I'm not trying to pay them back."

"Then what are you doing? I've noticed you are never idle. Which I do not mean as a criticism."

They stood looking at the water rippling by. She considered his words. "I simply believe in working as hard as I can."

Walker didn't say anything for several seconds, and she hoped he had abandoned the subject. "Mr. Bates says a powerful lot in a few words, doesn't he?"

She chuckled. "He surely does. What did you think of his message?"

"It was good. You know, he spoke to me last night. He asked questions and said things that I might object to from anyone else."

She studied him, wondering what Mr. Bates had said, hoping Walker would tell her.

His smile was lopsided. "He thinks I am carrying bitterness in my heart."

"Toward your uncle?"

He blinked. "So, you think it too?"

"I was only guessing, but it seems he struck a nerve."

"He also said I was afraid to plan a future."

She shivered at the thought of him wandering about aimlessly from one place to another. "Why did he say that?"

"I don't know."

"Is he right?"

Walker held her gaze with such intensity that her eyes watered. "I wouldn't say I'm afraid, but maybe I don't see how a person can expect permanency."

"I hope you are wrong. I intend to have a home that no one can take away." She needed to get that dress finished and, hopefully, attract some of the fancier ladies. "Did you tell Mr. Bates that?"

Walker gave a mirthless laugh. "He said something to the effect that I should plan and trust God for the outcome."

"Sounds like what Pa says to me. I try to explain it isn't that I don't trust God, but I think I need to do my part."

They studied each other. Josie felt as if they had ventured across a bridge meant only for them.

He smiled, filling his eyes with brightness. "So, as well as having uncles who let us down, we share a caution about the future?"

They sat on the grass. He identified the songs of several birds in the trees behind them. Along the bank was a patch of yellow flowers.

She pointed to them. "Pa calls those hairy cat's ear."

Walker laughed. He reached out and plucked a stem and examined it. "Looks like a tall dandelion to me." He handed her the flower, and she turned it about in her hand.

"Are you afraid of the future?" she asked.

"I wouldn't say it was fear that I feel. More like an unwillingness to repeat a painful lesson."

She assumed he was talking about the sale of the ranch his father and uncle had owned. "It must have been hard."

"I think it was the worst day of my life when Pa and Uncle Paul announced they were selling the ranch." He leaned back on his elbow as he talked, and Josie scooted around so she could watch the play of emotions on his face.

"Uncle Paul said he was taking his half of the money and going west. Pa said we were going to stay in Texas, but we soon moved away. I demanded to know why they were doing that. Hadn't they always told me that someday I would be a partner with them? They wouldn't say why they were doing what they were doing. Just that things change, and they couldn't keep their promise. I was so angry. It still hurts to think of the places I loved back there. I had a special place where I would often go. It was about half a mile from the house…a rocky prominence that allowed me a view of the land." A look of peace and longing filled his face.

"I'd climb to the top and sit in the shade of the only tree up there. The red rocks tumbled down the slope to stunted-looking bushes then the view opened up to a wide vista that seemed to have no beginning and no end. Often streaks of clouds crossed the sky. I could see forever from there. I thought it would always be where I went to think and dream."

He looked into the distance, his expression no longer peaceful. "I went to that spot just before we left and sat for a long time. Uncle Paul found me there and said it was time to leave. He said he regretted that things had turned out this way.

"I was angry and said they didn't have to.

"He said he had no choice. I wanted to know why. What had changed? But he wouldn't say.

Walker's expression had gone from pain to anger, but suddenly, went to surprise. "I just remembered that Uncle Paul told me he wanted to hear from me. I wonder if he still does or if he was simply trying to make me feel better at the moment."

"But you are going to see him, aren't you?"

"I promised my ma." The regret in his voice told Josie it was the only reason he was making the effort. "So that's why I have a hard time believing a home, a place, can be anything but temporary."

She nodded. "I can see why you would feel that way. But it's the opposite of how I feel." She looked past him, trying to sort out her feelings. "Mr. Bates talks like trusting God for the future is all a person needs." Realizing what she'd said, she gulped. "That makes me sound like an infidel."

"I don't think so. I think you're a little like me... Something happened in your past that seems to control your future. Like Mr. Bates said, we cling to things like unforgiveness and bitterness. Or blame and shame. I guess for me, it's blame. What is it for you?"

She forced herself not to jump to her feet and rush away as shame washed over her. Pa was such a respected man. If the community knew of her past, it would destroy his good name.

And hers.

She rose slowly and, she hoped, casually. "I need to get back in case Ma needs anything."

CHAPTER 8

*W*alker sprang to his feet and fell in at her side. "I didn't mean to pry. Forgive me and forget it."

"There's nothing to forgive."

He wanted to disagree. Something in his question had sent her hurrying toward home. Only because he thought they were being open and honest with each other did he probe into her reasons. He'd confessed his hurt and the blame he carried for so long. Though he wasn't sure whom he should blame. None of the adults had told him the real reason behind the sale of the ranch and the breakup of the partnership. "I guess I blame Uncle Paul the most. Because he left. I don't suppose that makes a lick of sense, but there it is."

"I understand."

"Good." But did she? They reached the house, and he stopped at the addition. "Good night. Call me if anything changes." He tipped his head toward the kitchen door.

Her eyes widened. "Do you think Pa might have a relapse?"

He squeezed his hands into fists. Why was he saying the wrong thing every time he turned around? "I think your pa is doing fine. Better than fine. I only meant my words as assurance that I'm here if you need anything."

"Oh. Well, thanks." She slipped inside and closed the door.

He thumped one fist on his forehead as he made his way to his cot. One thing he'd learned—don't ask personal questions of Josie. The knowledge was so much like how it had been with his uncle and parents that he promised himself he would do his best to ignore her except for meals and necessity.

OVER THE NEXT few days he learned it was easier to plan to avoid her than it was to actually accomplish it. Of course, they sat at the same table for meals. Mrs. Kinsley had ordered her husband not to work on the addition, and he seemed content enough to sit on a chair in the sunshine and read his Bible. But at meal times, he demanded a detailed report on the progress.

Walker told Jacob when he finished shingling the roof, when he installed the rest of the windows, and when he began work on the interior walls.

Jacob nodded with each report. "We need cupboards in the workroom and some low tables for the washtubs. I've ordered a stove too."

The next day he listed the things the bedrooms would need. "Shelves, a wardrobe, and bed frames. I've ordered lumber for them."

Walker began to suspect that Jacob wasn't spending as much time reading the Good Book as he was thinking of things for Walker to do. Not that Walker minded. He'd decided not to leave until he heard from his uncle and, of course, not until he had earned enough to buy a horse and outfit.

The elder couple were never far from each other. And retired to bed early, as did Stella and her children, though often Donny was allowed to stay up with Walker and Josie. Every evening Walker was faced with isolating himself in his room, trotting away without asking Josie to accompany him, or following his heart and walking with her. He chose the latter despite his resolve to keep their association to what was necessary.

On one of their outings, rather than walk by the river, Josie said she wanted to go past the schoolhouse.

"Looks brand new," Walker observed.

"It was finished earlier this year, but there have never been classes. Victoria was planning to teach, but she got married instead. Pa says a new teacher will be here in time to start classes in September."

"Ah," Donny moaned. "Ma will make me go. Unless—" He brightened. "Maybe we'll be back at the farm, and I won't have to attend. Sure hope so."

"Do you want to see inside?" Josie asked. At Walker's nod, she opened the door. They stood in a small cloak-room with rows of hooks and a bench. Beyond was the empty classroom.

"There are no desks or books." How would a teacher work in such a situation?

"Some of the men are making desks. Books..." She

paused. "Maybe we'll have to have a fund raiser to get enough money to buy what we need."

"Why do you look so troubled about that?"

"The community gave so much to build the school. I don't know if they will be able to give more."

"Maybe they would if they thought they'd get something special in return."

She tipped her head to consider him. "Did you have something in mind?"

"Maybe." The idea formed slowly. "This is ranching and farming country. Lots of cowboys and would-be cowboys. Why not have a rodeo?"

"What's that?" Donny asked.

"It's a competition to see which cowboy can do certain things the fastest or the best. Like roping, riding a wild horse...stuff like that. I watched some men one time seeing who could stay on the back of a wild bull the longest." He chuckled. "None of them lasted very long."

"It sounds dangerous."

"Not really. Most of the games are things that cowboys do all the time."

Her eyebrows rose. "They ride bulls?"

"It's an exercise to prove how brave one is."

"Or how foolish." Her eyes narrowed. "Have you taken part in such foolishness?"

He chuckled. "I might have."

"I took you for having more sense than that."

He laughed. "It was fun even though I got tossed in the dirt."

"I could ride a bull," Donny said with conviction.

"Your ma might not let you." Walker hoped that would be enough to stop Donny's interest. He turned back to Josie. "It could bring in enough money for books. Contestants would pay for a chance to compete, and you'd charge an admission fee for people to watch. What do you think?"

"I'll ask Pa. Actually, *we'll* ask him." A spark of interest in her eyes told him she liked the idea more than she let on.

"It's a great idea." He pulled her arm through his and marched them back to the house. He stepped into the addition, and she and Donny went into the house.

THE NEXT MORNING he joined the others at breakfast.

Donny sat at Walker's side. "You gonna ask him now?"

Every eye turned toward Walker. He hadn't planned to make it a public request, but why not? It would require everyone's support. "Jacob, I saw the schoolhouse yesterday. Josie says there's a teacher coming soon."

Donny groaned and earned a warning look from his mother.

Walker continued. "I understand there is a need for books and supplies. I have an idea that might bring in enough money to purchase them. A rodeo." He hurried on with his explanation.

When he finished, Jacob nodded thoughtfully. "It sounds like a decent plan. Let me talk to the other board members, and I'll let you know what we decide. How long do you think it would take to organize such an event?"

Walker lifted his hands. "I have no idea. I've never

planned an event of any sort." He looked around the table. "Have any of you?"

Josie grinned. "We've done a few things."

"Perfect," Jacob said. "The two of you can be in charge. I'll talk to the others today and let you know."

Walker swallowed loudly, hoping no one would notice. He had just talked himself into very unfamiliar territory. It was one thing to participate in a rodeo, quite another to organize it— especially with the woman he had vowed to keep his distance from. But he couldn't deny a tiny bubble of anticipation at the thought of working with her.

Breakfast over, Jacob asked his wife to accompany him to visit the other board members.

Stella carried a basket of knitting outside. The two children accompanied her.

As Walker prepared to leave the kitchen and return to his work on the addition, Josie spoke his name softly.

"Pa approves, so likely the others will," she said.

"I know I suggested it, but I've never planned a rodeo. The ones I took part in happened spur of the moment."

Her smile was reassuring. "We'll pull it together."

"Or die trying," he muttered.

She laughed.

He glowered at her, not knowing what amused her so.

She sobered and wiped her eyes. "I don't see planning the event as the dangerous part. Isn't that relegated to riding wild animals?"

He grinned as he went out to hang one of the doors on the addition. He listened for the Kinsleys to return. Josie seemed certain the idea would be approved. As he worked, he tried not to imagine evenings spent with

Josie as they sat, heads bent together, working out details of the rodeo.

He was about to put up a door when he realized he had hung the hinges on the wrong side. He groaned and took down his work. He needed to keep his mind on what he was doing and not let it wander down paths filled with imaginary scenes.

* * *

JOSIE WANTED to rush to the door when she heard Ma and Pa return but forced herself to remain at the cupboard, putting away dishes. It wasn't as if she was anxious to hear what the board had decided. Just as she wasn't hoping for a legitimate excuse to spend time with Walker, even though she could not answer all his questions about her past or her dreams for the future.

However, it would be nice to earn enough money to buy books for the school.

Her thoughts slammed into a wall. Wasn't she supposed to be concentrating on finishing her dress and building up her sewing business so she could be independent? Secure? She would bring the garment down and work on it every chance she got.

Ma led Pa into the kitchen, and he sank wearily into the nearest chair. His face was pale. The skin around his eyes tight. Josie's worry was reflected in Ma's eyes. She regretted her eagerness to plan a rodeo. Pa shouldn't have gone out when he wasn't feeling well yet. It had been selfish on her part to let him. Even encourage him.

"Pa, I'm sorry I let you go out." She set the kettle to boil.

He waved a hand. "I don't recall needing your permission. Young Walker has a good idea, and I don't see any reason to delay getting it into play." He sighed. "I didn't realize how weak I am."

Ma sat beside him, rubbing his hands. "Now, Jacob, you are going to rest until these weak spells pass. There's nothing that Josie and Walker and I can't handle. Thank God for sending that young man our way when He did."

Josie kept her back to them as she poured hot water over the tea leaves. She put out cups and cookies and waited for the brew to steep. Donny must have a sixth sense about food because he rushed in and sat at the table, eyeing the cookies.

Stella and Blossom followed more slowly, but Blossom was soon sitting at the table next to her brother.

Chuckling, Josie poured them each a glass of milk and offered them cookies. She put out another cup for Stella and poured tea for all the adults. She didn't sit at the table with the others. Instead, she remained where she could see out the window.

Walker appeared in the doorway of the addition and glanced toward the house. She knew he couldn't see her, but still her eyes warmed at the impatience in his face. It seemed he was as eager to have his idea approved as she was. Though perhaps for entirely different reasons.

What was her reason? Only to buy books for the school, she told herself. There was absolutely no other reason, and to prove it to herself, she filled a cup with tea and sat at the table. She took a cookie and ate it, though it was strangely flavorless.

How foolish she was becoming. She gave herself a

mental shake. The lessons she'd learned while in the care of her uncle could not be forgotten.

Pa drank his tea. His color improved.

Josie would not ask what the board had decided. She told herself it mattered not one way or the other. But when Pa addressed her, she couldn't pretend her heart didn't give an excited leap.

"Josie, the board is one hundred percent in support of having a rodeo and said to thank Walker for the suggestion.

"That's nice." She hoped her voice revealed only moderate interest.

"Norm, at the store, suggests you make some handbills, and he'll pass them out to everyone who comes in. And of course, a poster." Pa chuckled as if he knew how hard she tried to pretend she wasn't pleased "Why don't you go tell Walker the good news?"

"I will." She rose slowly, crossed the room in measured steps, and went outside where she paused to draw in a deep breath. Then, smiling widely, she hurried to the addition. She paused inside the doorway. "Walker?"

"Here." He came through one of the doors. "You look pleased."

"The board approves having a rodeo." She passed on their thanks and the idea of handbills.

Walker raked his fingers through his hair. "How long do we have?"

"I don't know. Pa didn't say." She might had forgotten to ask.

"Tell me how we organize this."

She laughed a little at his worry. "First, we need a

date. Then we make the handbills and posters. I guess before that, we have to decide on events."

"I'm beginning to think I should have kept my mouth shut."

She patted his arm. "Walker, we can do this." She looked about the room. "Can you leave your work for a bit so we can get started?"

He looked about to refuse then sucked in air. "I guess I have no one to blame but myself." He squared his shoulders. "Lead on, fair lady."

"Let's ask Pa if they set a date."

They returned to the house. Stella and the children had gone out, but Ma and Pa still sat at the table.

"Pa, did anyone suggest a date?"

"Yes, they did. Didn't I mention it? Norm pointed out that the teacher is due to arrive in four weeks. He said if we had the books by the time he arrives, it would let the man see that we are serious about our children's education. Norm said it would take a couple of weeks to get the shipment, so he said we must have the rodeo in two weeks' time. That should be plenty of time to plan."

Josie nodded. "We'll have to get right at it."

"Walker, put it ahead of the addition," Pa said.

Josie headed for the parlor. "Come on, Walker. We have work to do."

He followed. "I confess I'm at a loss."

She pulled out the little table the family often used to do jigsaw puzzles or play games. She pulled a chair to one side, and he did the same across the table. Before she sat, she got paper, pencils, a pen, and a bottle of ink from the desk. "Okay, the first thing we need is a list." She poised her pencil above the paper.

"Go head. Write," he said.

She glanced up, saw the teasing light in his eyes. "You think I'm bluffing?"

"Are you?"

She chuckled. "I think I will have to depend on your expertise when it comes to the events. Tell me what we should have."

He nodded and, as he talked, she wrote.

Wild horse riding

Steer wrestling

Team roping

Horse races

Wild cow milking.

She stopped writing to stare at him. "Wild cow milking. What is that?"

He grinned, his eyes brimming with amusement. "It's a lot of fun. Teams of four, all on foot, have to rope and restrain a cow so one of the members can milk it. The first team to do so is the winner." He chuckled. "The cows are off the range and not used to being handled, let alone milked. It's wild."

She narrowed her eyes. "Isn't it dangerous?"

He sobered. "It might be for a greenhorn, but these are cowboys who are used to dealing with cows."

"I beg your pardon. I hadn't realized being a cowboy eliminated danger." She kept her face expressionless but hoped he'd be able to tell she was teasing.

"Doesn't eliminate it, of course. But cowboys are tough." He drew himself up tall and looked down his nose at her. "Invincible, even."

She half rose and leaned over to tap his head where she knew it was still tender from being hit with a pistol. "Seems to me you might be exaggerating."

He barely managed not to blink. "There might be some exceptions," he said in a wounded tone.

She sank back to her chair and picked up her pencil. "Any more events?"

"It would be nice if there was a trick roper."

She grinned. "You have two weeks to perfect the skill."

He guffawed. "Maybe if I had two years." He grew thoughtful. "I once knew a man who could do all sorts of tricks. I wonder where he is now. Wouldn't it be great if we could find him?"

"Walker. I assume we will have the rodeo on a Saturday. That gives us fifteen days. There isn't time to hunt down an old acquaintance." She bent over the paper again. "Now I'll begin a list of what we need to do."

Handbills

Posters

Set entry fees and admission price

"Guess that needs to be first."

Where to hold it.

"Will there be prizes for the winners?" she asked.

"I suppose so."

She added it to the list and looked up. "Anything else?"

"You tell me. You're the expert."

"Not at rodeos. I think that will do. I hope someone will let us know if we've left anything out." They discussed fees, admission, and prizes, and then she cut paper into quarters.

She put the ink bottle between them and gave him a

pen. "We need handbills. The more the better, I suppose. Norm can hand them out at the store. I'm sure we can get Jimmy and Mickey to give them out at the livery barn and Sylvie at the diner." She began to print letters. *Glory Rodeo. Come one, come all. Money raised goes to buy books for the school.* She listed the events, the costs, and the date.

Walker had not written a thing.

"Something wrong?"

"Nope. But we better make sure our handbills say the same thing." He took her finished product and carefully copied the words.

Josie smiled at the way he chewed his bottom lip in concentration. She studied him a moment. One thing she'd noted about him was the effort he put into whatever he worked at. He measured carefully before he cut a length of wood. He aligned things exactly. He always put in a solid day's work.

How often in the last couple of years she was with her uncle had she tried to convince him it would take less effort to make an honest living than it required to cheat and steal and con others. He'd laughed and said it wasn't half as much fun.

She must have sighed, for Walker looked at her. His expression grew serious.

"Something wrong?"

She shivered. "No. Just an unwelcome memory."

"Wanna tell me about it?" His gaze was warm and inviting.

She thought of all the times she'd ached to tell someone what her prior life had been like. Longed for someone to ease away her regrets and shame. Yes, she knew God forgave her. But she walked through life knowing she would carry her guilt until she reached heaven when God would finally lift the burden from her shoulders. The words raced to her tongue, but she clamped her teeth together to hold them back. There was far too much to lose by confessing. Not only Walker's friendship but her parents' reputation in the community. Her own acceptance.

She shook her head. "Just one of those things that comes and goes from time to time."

His gaze did not falter. "If you ever feel the need to talk, I'm a fair, good listener." He gave a pleased look. "My Ma said so."

She chuckled. "Then it must be so."

"You won't forget it?"

"I won't." Not even if she tried. And she intended to. Just as she intended to keep her past hidden even though it meant she must guard her heart against her growing attraction to Walker.

He was everything she didn't want—homeless, a drifter, honest.

And everything she did want—kind, fun, and honest.

Wanting did not make such things possible for her.

CHAPTER 9

*W*alker watched the play of emotions on Josie's face. Her mouth worked as she appeared to fight an inner battle. It was plain to see that something about the unexpected memory had upset her. He wanted to touch her, soothe her, and assure her that her memories had no hold on her. But he was reluctant to startle her. She promised to remember he was a good listener, but the way she drew in air and stilled her face to reveal nothing, he guessed she would not be confiding in him any time soon.

She picked up her forgotten pen and bent over the piece of paper. "We have a lot of these to do and not much time to do them."

He returned his attention to printing the notices. It was slow work for him because he wanted the announcement to be neat. As he worked, memories came to his mind too, and he began to talk.

"I attended school in town one year only. Other than that, my parents taught me my lessons." He chuckled. "I wonder if the teacher wished I had stayed out in the country." He grew thoughtful as he remembered those difficult days. "It was right after the ranch had been sold. Pa hadn't decided what to do yet, so we lived in town, and he helped out at the feed store. I was not happy to be stuck in town and didn't mind letting everyone know that I thought it was unfair."

His hands had grown still, and he noticed Josie's had as well. Her gaze was riveted to him. He tried to smile but couldn't force his lips to obey him.

"The ranch meant a lot to you, didn't it?"

"You could say that." He heard the bitter note in his voice. "I know it's over and done with, but to this day, I regret that they sold it. I guess at that point I felt homeless."

"Perhaps you still do. Could it be the reason you don't see yourself settling down?"

He hadn't ever thought of it, but now that he did, it made perfect sense. "Guess I don't expect to ever feel that sense of belonging and...I don't know...maybe ownership, I felt back then."

"So, it's easier to keep moving."

"It has been." Their gazes locked as a new thought grew inside his head and in his heart. "Maybe I needed something or someone to make me feel like I could settle."

She held his gaze a moment longer, no doubt seeing the truth of what he said. That he might find a reason here to put down roots right here. She blinked, and he felt an invisible door slap shut between them.

"I hope you find it," she murmured.

Did their growing attraction mean nothing to her? Or

was he mistaken in thinking it was mutual? Was his penniless, homeless state so important that she couldn't see who he was?

Down the hall, a door slammed. A pot banged with a metallic twang as someone set it on the stove.

"Oh my." Josie pushed to her feet. "I should be helping with the meal." She rushed toward the door then returned to cover the ink. She wiped both pens and set aside the dry handbills. "I guess we'll have to finish these later."

She swept from the room.

He followed more slowly. He couldn't help but notice she didn't say when later would be.

They were about to sit down for dinner when the sound of horse hooves drew Josie to the window. "It's Flora. She's leading a horse."

Jacob joined her at the window. "I wonder what she's up to."

They watched for a moment, then Jacob returned to the table.

Josie went to the cupboard. "I'll set a place for her." She put out another set of dishes, all the while avoiding looking at Walker.

It pained him that she so thoroughly shut him out.

Flora burst through the door. "Pa, I brought you a new horse." She looked around the table, greeting each one. Her gaze stopped at Josie.

Walker wondered what she saw. Then she looked at him. "Got another horse you might be interested in. He'd be just right for you." She sat at the place prepared for her.

"I'll bear that in mind." He needed to earn more

money before he could purchase a horse. Not that he minded taking time away from his labors to work on the rodeo plan.

"We're going to have a rodeo," Donny announced as soon as he got a chance to speak.

"That a fact?" Flora looked around the table and satisfied it was, she asked, "Whose idea is this?"

"Walker's." Donny beamed with pride to be the one to say so.

Flora demanded all the information. Walker filled her in.

"Horse races?" she said. "I'll be entering that one."

Jacob began to protest.

Flora held her palm up. "With Kade's approval, of course."

Her pa sat back, a resigned look on his face.

"Nice of you to bring a horse," Mrs. Kinsley said, likely hoping to shift the conversation to a less treacherous topic. "But your father isn't up to riding just yet."

"That's fine. He can make friends with the horse first. Always a good move."

The meal ended, and Flora and Josie began to clean the kitchen. Walker guessed there would be no more work done on notices today and returned to the addition. There was still plenty to do—doors to hang, shelves and cupboards to make and, as soon as it arrived, a stove to install.

He could see out two windows and the outside door as he worked. Josie and Flora walked by, Donny hard on their heels. Where were they going? He leaned to the side. They passed the garden and turned down the back street. Were they going to visit friends?

Over the days and especially at church, he'd seen lots of young men and women, older ones too, speaking to Josie and her sisters. But was there someone special? A male friend? He jerked back to his work and hammered in a nail with extra vigor. It wasn't as if he cared. Besides, hadn't she made it clear that first day that she wasn't interested in anyone?

And if she was, it would not be a penniless, homeless cowboy.

Maybe he'd get a job nearby and make a lot of money and buy himself a ranch. One as nice as the one he thought would be his back in Texas.

He laughed at his convoluted thinking. His only plans were to find his uncle, deliver the message he'd promised his ma to deliver, and then…

And then?

He couldn't give an answer. Rather than dwell on it, he set about measuring and planning a cupboard for the workroom.

A little later, he looked up at the sound of voices. It was Mr. and Mrs. Kinsley going to look at the new horse. Walker watched. A fine-looking animal—a light bay with a proud carriage. He would ask Flora what the other horse looked like.

He heard her voice and saw that the two girls had joined their parents. Flora was telling her pa about the horse.

Walker made up his mind to speak to Flora and jogged over to join them. "Tell me about the other horse you have."

"He's a dark bay gelding. Beautiful horse. I didn't

want to part with him, but I have two more youngsters coming up and can't keep all of them."

"He's a good horse? Strong? Good for long days carrying a man?"

"He's a big, well-muscled horse. I trained him and broke him. So, he's the best there is." She spoke with some heat.

He chuckled. "I'm not arguing. Could you save him for me?"

"I sure don't mind keeping him around." She quirked her eyebrows at him. "You planning to leave soon?"

"I need to earn enough money to buy him and the necessary tack I need."

"Huh." Her gaze went to Josie and then returned to him. She studied him a moment. He steeled himself to reveal nothing.

"Huh," she said again.

He stole a quick glance at Josie, but she seemed completely consumed with watching the horse.

"What are you going to call him, Pa?" Josie asked.

"I'm sure Flora has named him, so I don't see any reason to change it. What's his name, Flora?"

"Tic." The horse pricked up his ears and whinnied.

"Tic?" Her pa looked surprised. "I didn't expect that."

Flora's cheek flared pink. "Well, I started out calling him Majestic, but that just got too hard to say, so I shortened it to Tic."

Her pa laughed. "Tic it is. Here, Tic." He held out a handful of oats to the horse, who looked at him warily and remained at a distance.

"He'll take his time," Flora said. "But once he's decided he likes you, he will be loyal." She climbed over the fence and went to the horse, petting him and saying good-bye, then jumped to her own mount. "I best get home. Kade misses me something awful when I'm gone." With a merry laugh, she rode away.

Walker realized he should have asked her what she'd named his horse. "I hope she didn't name the other horse a sissy name like Sue. I once knew of a man who had a horse named that, and it got so he couldn't say the animal's name around any of the cowboys."

* * *

JOSIE LAUGHED HARDER at the idea of naming a horse Sue than the comment deserved. It was her nerves. She continually struggled to control her feelings about Walker, and it put her on edge. Just when she was beginning to think he might be the kind of man who would give her the security she sought, he did something to remind her he didn't mean to settle. Like talking about buying a horse from Flora. *Good for long days carrying a man.* That meant only one thing. Walker meant to ride north. Perhaps he would never settle down.

Not that it mattered. She had her own plans. She hurried to the house and up the stairs to get her sewing basket. She carried it down to the kitchen. Ma and Pa had returned, and Walker hovered in the doorway. Stella had gone back outside, taking her knitting with her.

Ma looked at Josie. "You're planning to sew?"

"I have to finish this dress. I'm going to ask Norm if I can display it in the store by the yard goods. If I can do that before the rodeo, lots of people will see it. I might get some work." She hadn't ever thought of hanging her dress in the store, but the words came out in a rush. It was a good idea. She should have thought of it before. An urgency to finish her garment made her rush to the table and pull out her needle and thread.

Pa cleared his throat.

Josie looked up.

"I thought there was some need to get handbills made. And a poster." His voice was gentle yet scolding.

"Oh, I guess it slipped my mind." She put the needle and thread back in the basket. "I'll do this later." She rose and glanced at Walker. "Shall we?" She led the way to the sitting room and resumed her place. In a few deft movements, she opened the ink and began printing another announcement.

Walker sat across from her, dipped his pen in the ink, and bent his head over his own bit of paper.

Tension made her hand jerk. The nib caught, and ink spattered across the page. She quickly blotted it, but the announcement was ruined.

She felt Walker's watchful interest, but kept her head bowed over the new piece of paper she began working on.

"Is something wrong?" he asked.

"Why do you ask?" She realized her reply gave him the right to continue asking questions. She should have simply said no and ended any further discussion.

"Do I really have to say? You're so tense you're almost tearing the paper."

She paused, trying to lighten her touch.

He set his pen down. "I don't know what I said to upset you, but whatever it was, it was unintentional. And

I'm sorry. If you'd rather I didn't help with printing these, I'll leave."

Josie scrambled for a reply. If he left, it would take her twice as long. She'd never get a chance to finish her dress. Besides, it would be lonely.

He pushed back from the table.

She lifted her head and met his gaze. Guarded. Full of regret. Her heart smote her. He hadn't said or done anything she should be upset about. He'd always been clear that he was moving on. Not ready to settle. Except he had hinted that the right place, the right person, would change his mind. She'd wondered if he meant her. But then he'd talked to Flora, and she realized she must have read more into his words than he meant.

He began to rise.

"I'll never finish these on my own. Please stay and help."

He studied her. His look went on and on.

She drew in a sharp breath. What did he think he saw? What did he hope to see? For the space of half a heartbeat, she thought of opening the doors to her secret. Her ribs refused to work. Her head started to pound for want of a breath.

He sighed. He'd wanted more but she'd disappointed him. "I am committed to helping you make this event successful." He sat down and began to print the letters.

He'd said the right things, but his words left her hollow inside. Alone. Fearful. Why must her past always haunt her?

They worked until she deemed it time to help with supper, although Ma had come to the room and said she and Stella were preparing it.

The pile of handbills was growing very slowly.

Walker looked at the stack too. "There aren't near enough to leave at three businesses. Shouldn't we have them done and delivered by Saturday so those coming to town can get them?"

"Definitely. We should probably deliver them tomorrow, so they'll be available to the early comers."

"I'll keep working and come back after supper."

"I'll come back too." It meant she wouldn't have the evening for sewing, but once these handbills were done, she'd concentrate on her project.

Walker stayed behind as she went to the kitchen.

When supper was ready, Donny ran down the hall to call him. As Walker came to the kitchen, he rubbed his neck and groaned. "Reminds me of why I didn't like school."

"I don't like it either," Donny said.

"How would you know?" His mother spoke gently. "You've never been."

Walker realized what he'd said. "Maybe it was only that I missed our ranch."

Stella gave him a grateful look.

Pa seemed weary and ate slowly.

Ma watched him carefully as did Josie. Before Pa finished his meal, Ma took the fork from his hand. "I think it's time for us to retire," she said.

When Pa didn't argue, Josie's concern shot up. She waited until her parents had gone to their room and closed the door to lean across the table and quietly address both Stella and Walker. "Shouldn't he be feeling better by now?"

Stella shrugged. "I ask the same question of myself. Seems the body sets its own schedule."

Josie shifted her gaze to Walker.

"Perhaps he just overdid it today."

She hoped he was right. The meal over, she hurriedly cleaned the kitchen while Walker went out to tend the horse, Donny at his side, talking nonstop.

Stella sighed. "That boy wears me out."

Blossom sat at the table turning the pages of a picture book.

"At least she's quieter." Stella sat by the cupboard and dried dishes.

"We have to make some more handbills," Josie said. "But we'll keep Donny with us."

"You're sure he won't get in the way?"

"I think we can handle him."

"Thank you."

As soon as the dishes were finished, Stella wearily made her way to her room, Blossom clinging to her hand. Josie looked around the kitchen. It was early. She had the entire evening to finish the handbills. It would have been a lonely task to do on her own.

Walker came through the door.

Thankfully, she didn't have to do it alone.

Perhaps her smile of welcome said more than she meant it to, because Walker ground to a halt, stared at her, and then grinned widely and said, "Seems you're eager to get those things done."

"I am." And it was the only reason for the lightness of her fickle heart. "Donny, you can come with us."

The boy raced ahead.

Josie found a basket holding a Noah's Ark and an

assortment of animals and put it by the table. Donny sat on the floor and began to play.

They worked diligently. Walker stretched often and rubbed his neck. Her neck began to ache too.

Josie glanced at the clock on the desk. "Donny, it's time for you to go to bed."

The boy put the animals and the ark away and slipped from the room.

Walker didn't suggest stopping, and neither did Josie. "We can deliver these tomorrow morning if we're done."

"My thoughts too." They both reached for a new piece of paper. Their hands collided, and she jerked back, giving a nervous laugh.

His eyebrows rose toward his hairline, and she knew he wondered at her strange behavior.

No more so than she did.

To cover up her nervousness, she began to talk. "I consider you fortunate to have been able to attend school."

"Didn't you?"

"When I joined the Kinsley family, I could neither read nor write. I'd never attended school. We moved around too much." She couldn't tell him how often she had been whisked from bed in the middle of the night as they made their escape.

"I see that changed." He jabbed his pen toward the printing she labored over.

"Ma taught me. She said there was no point in me attending classes. They would put me with the little kids, and she didn't consider that appropriate. I struggled to read at first, but once the letters made sense, Ma said there was no slowing me down. And I discovered I loved putting letters on paper and seeing words grow."

Walker continued to work as he spoke. "I didn't mind learning. Like I said, I think half my objection to school was I saw it as somehow connected to losing the ranch."

"Donny might feel that way too." She told him of the many times the boy said he wanted to go back to their farm.

"Then for his sake, I hope it happens."

"Me too." Josie smiled at him as they shared a wish for the child. "Stella would like to return, but she simply isn't well enough yet."

"She's fortunate to end up with the Kinsleys."

Josie nodded. "I agree. So am I. When I think—" She didn't finish. Couldn't bear to think what her life would have become if she'd stayed with her uncle. She grew thoughtful as she remembered some early memories. "One of the happiest days of my life was an Easter morning. I had been with the Kinsleys two or three months and no longer feared that Uncle would come for me. We were all given new dresses to wear to church. Mine was a blue cotton with ruffles around the sleeves and the collar." She chuckled.

"I imagine it was pretty plain, but it was the nicest dress I could remember having. I helped Ma stitch it together, and it was my pride and joy."

She leaned back, her task momentarily forgotten. "Each of us girls wore a dress we had helped sew. I thought we looked really fine. My uncle had always cut my hair because he said it was easier to tend, but it had grown out and hung to my shoulders. It was fixed back with combs. I remember the bubbling joy inside me that was quite the opposite of the fear I'd known most of my life. It was a day that I saw only the future with a family who loved me and cared for me. They gave me meals and a warm bed and so much more. Pa preached a sermon about Christ's resurrection and reminded us that because He lives, we can face whatever lies before us. That day I decided I would look forward, not back. I would no longer fear my uncle. I would take advantage of every opportunity that came my way to create a life that provided me with security. Most of all, I would never forget the kindness shown to me by Ma and Pa Kinsley."

She realized how long she'd been talking and how much she had revealed. Above all, she realized that she had made little progress in looking only to the future. The past still held her.

Walker's hands had grown still, and he studied her. His gaze sought her hidden secrets, and she almost let them flow out.

"What were you afraid of?" he asked, his voice so low it was like the purr of a cat and, just like a friendly cat, it asked for more. "Did your uncle hurt you?"

"He didn't beat me, if that's what you mean."

He waited.

She couldn't tear her gaze from his. How often she had yearned to spill the secrets of her heart. She drew in air until her lungs could hold no more.

Some secrets could not be shared. Why was she having to remind herself of that so often these last few days?

"He lived a wandering way of life. I never knew if I would go to sleep in the same bed I woke up in or if we would move." Let Walker think that was all there was to it. She returned to penning the letters.

"That's sad."

The evening shadows filled the room, and Walker lit a lamp and set it between them.

Ma stepped into the room, wearing a robe. "I saw a light on. How much longer will you work?"

Josie eyed the growing pile of handbills. "We need to deliver these around town tomorrow. And we haven't made the posters yet."

"Very well. But don't forget you need your sleep." Ma hesitated, perhaps wondering if she should remain in the room and chaperone. "I'll leave my bedroom door open." Her warning was loud and clear. She'd be listening for any inappropriate activity.

"We'll be fine, Ma. Don't worry about us." All she had in mind was finishing up this task.

There could be nothing more, even if her heart ached for it.

CHAPTER 10

*W*alker heard Mrs. Kinsley's gentle warning. Just as he saw Josie's hard resistance to his questions. Yet he had detected something more in Josie's eyes when she talked about feeling safe with the Kinsleys and being afraid with her uncle. He understood how losing a home could do that to a person, but he knew from the way her eyes darted away from his as she spoke that there was more to it than that. Her voice was firm when she said her uncle hadn't beaten her. He was not ignorant about the many other ways a man could hurt a child, and he shuddered.

As if sensing how his thoughts circled around her words, Josie began to speak. "I was fortunate that I didn't have to go to school with the other girls. Ma spent more time with me and taught me to sew. I loved creating pretty garments. I still do. I'm going to take in more orders and make enough to buy a sewing machine. Then I'm going to buy a little shop and have my own business.

I'll live in the back of the shop. It will be my home." Her voice carried a note of determination as she spoke of her dream.

"You have a name for this business?"

She flashed him a look that was half embarrassed, half proud. "Josie's Creations."

"Sounds like you've given this a lot of thought."

"For about the last five years. When we moved here, I knew it would take more work to get enough customers. Not like back in Ohio, where there were lots of people and lots of fancily dressed women." She sighed. "Do you think the ranchers to the west will learn of the rodeo and come?"

"If they hear about it, I expect they will. All cowboys like to show off their skills. Why? You thinking of sewing fancy shirts for them?"

She stared. "I never thought of it, but there's no reason I couldn't. If I'd thought of it sooner, I could have one sewn."

"You still have a couple of weeks."

"True." Another frustrated sigh. "What I had in mind was perhaps the ranchers would bring their wives and daughters, and I'd get some orders."

"Sounds like a feasible plan." He counted the handbills. "A hundred. That should be enough to divide up for the three businesses."

"Now for posters. What shall we do?"

They discussed ideas, and she began to pencil out a rough sketch. They hunkered over it, both making suggestions until they were satisfied.

"We'll need at least three," she said.

"Why don't you outline them, and I'll fill them in?"

"Good idea. We have colored pencils that will make it brighter." She got them from the desk. As she drew out the first poster, he bundled the handbills into three piles and tied each with a length of string.

He pulled his chair around to sit beside her as she finished the first poster, and then he carefully colored it. Several times he sat back to study his work.

She looked over at his work. "It's going to look very nice." She rubbed her neck and rolled her head. "My goodness. Look at the time."

He glanced at the clock. "Almost midnight. Do you want to stop?"

"No. We need to finish. But there's no need for you to stay."

"More hands, less work. I'll stay." But he would work faster even if it wasn't as good as he'd like. He finished the first poster and took the second from her. She drew the third one and began to color it.

Half an hour later, they finished.

He rose and stretched. There was no need to linger and lots of reasons to leave immediately, not the least of which was they were both tired. "Good night," he said, and strode from the room. He passed her parents' bedroom. The door was still open.

"Good night, Walker." Mrs. Kinsley's voice was low.

Had she lain awake all this time in order to protect her daughter's honor? Walker smiled. Both at how protective they were and how unnecessary it was. Most times Josie wore invisible armor that warned away unwanted advances. But on rare occasions, he thought he detected a crack in that armor. Calling a quiet good night, he went to the door.

"Good night, Ma," Josie called, and headed for the stairs.

It had been a long evening. Before they knew it, morning would dawn.

* * *

THE NEXT MORNING, as soon as breakfast was over, Walker and Josie took the posters and handbills and headed for Main Street. Their first stop was White's Store.

"Can you hand these out?" Josie gave Norm a stack of handbills.

He examined them. "These look nice. I hope we have a good turnout."

A young woman ventured into the store from the back room and greeted Josie.

Josie waved her forward. "Have you meet Walker Jones? He's helping Pa and now is in charge of organizing a rodeo. Walker, this is Lisa Walton." Walker had seen the young woman at church but hadn't been formally introduced.

"My sister-in-law." Norm's smile said he was proud of the fact.

Walker handed Norm the poster. "Can we hang this?"

"There's a board outside where everyone will see it." He reached under the counter and pulled out a tack hammer and four tacks. "Here you go."

Walker went out to secure the paper to the board. He

finished and was ready to return inside, when he heard Lisa talking. He assumed to Josie.

"Looks like you got your own cowboy. Just like your sisters."

Walker stopped and strained to hear Josie's answer.

"He's planning to leave as soon as he can." The words sounded harsh and final.

Walker drew back. Had he really given the impression that he was anxious to leave?

Was he?

Josie continued speaking, but Walker realized she addressed Norm. "Can I hang a couple samples of my sewing in your store and a notice that I am taking orders?"

"Certainly," Norm said. "I'm happy to help you out."

"Tsk." Lisa's displeasure was clear. "Are you still planning to stay rooted here in town? No desire to look further afield?"

"I haven't changed my mind." Josie's voice was soft, but Walker heard the firmness behind her words.

"There's so much more out there."

Walker took a step closer to the door and saw Lisa wave her arms as if to include the whole world.

Josie chuckled. "I'm quite happy here." She shifted her attention back to Norm. "Thanks. I'll get to work on the garments I want to display." She turned, saw Walker, and bade good-bye to the others.

They fell into step as they went down the street to Sylvie's Diner.

"Coffee? Breakfast?" Sylvie called. "Got some nice muffins still warm from the oven."

129

"I know the muffins would be delicious," Josie said. "But we've come about the rodeo."

Sylvie huffed over to where they stood. "Heard about it. What can I do to help?" She eyed Walker as she talked, her gaze darting to Josie and back to Walker.

He wondered what was going through her head. He didn't have to wait long to find out.

"Hope you plan to rope this good-looking cowboy before the rodeo. I expect the town will fill up with girls looking to hogtie a man."

Walker couldn't say who blushed the brightest, but his cheeks felt like they were on fire. "I don't aim to let anyone hogtie me," he managed to blurt out.

The color receded in Josie's cheeks. "He's got plans to move on."

Why did she have to say that so often? The thought was sour.

Sylvie looked like she wanted to shake Walker. "Not the staying sort?" Then her face softened into a smile. "Men change their minds. Why, look at Earl. He comes to town every chance he gets and says he plans to move in for good this winter."

"I'm glad for you," Josie said. She held out a packet of handbills. "Can you give these out to people who come into the diner?"

Sylvie took the handbills and looked at them. "I'll see that everyone gets one. It sounds like fun. I've been thinking about it. How about I serve coffee and charge for each cup? I can add that to the funds for the schoolbooks."

"Excellent idea." Josie and Walker spoke at the same time, glanced at each other, and grinned.

Then, realizing how closely Sylvie watched them, Walker shifted and pretended a great interest in the far table.

"Walker has a poster that we'd like to display here as well."

He jerked his attention back to the task at hand and presented Sylvie with a poster.

"I'll put in on the door so it can't be missed," she said.

"Thank you," he said, and hurried from the diner. As soon as they were out of earshot, he said, "That woman has see-all eyes."

Josie chuckled. "You might be right. Between her and Mickey and young Jimmy there isn't much that happens in town without one of them taking note."

"And having an opinion?"

"They're kind-hearted."

He laughed. "So are you."

She grinned at him, her eyes warm. "Nice of you to see it that way."

They crossed the street and went down the block, turned right, and went to the big red barn. "Not often you see a barn painted so red," he commented.

"Mickey wanted to spruce up the place. He was trying to impress Jimmy's ma."

"Did it work?"

"Seems to have. They are now married."

"Wow. So, it's red paint a man needs." He held her gaze, teasing and challenging her at the same time.

"I wouldn't suggest it would work for every woman." They had stopped walking and faced each other at the corner of the fence penning in the livery barn horses.

"What would work for you?" He shouldn't have asked

the question, knowing she wanted more than he could offer. Maybe more than any man could, unless she let go of the past and trusted in a good future.

The minute grew long and pulsed with promise and—

He was about to say, hope. Dare he admit his hopes? To get a ranch? To understand why his father had sold their ranch?

She sucked in a deep breath and looked at the horses. "Nothing anyone can offer me. I aim to take care of myself."

He heard words she didn't speak. "Because you can trust no one but yourself?"

By the way she jerked he knew his words had touched a nerve. Then she shook herself as if shaking them off. "I trust Ma and Pa and my sisters."

"Glad to hear it." The finality of her words said she'd never allow herself to trust anyone else. Except—"What about your brothers-in-law?"

"So far, so good." She forged ahead to the barn.

So far, so good? That wasn't trust at all.

He followed her. Mickey saw them and came over to greet them.

He agreed to hand out the handbills and display the poster. "Say, where are you getting the stock?" He addressed Walker.

"Stock?" How had they gotten this far in planning a rodeo, and he'd never even thought of that small detail? Small? Hardly. Without animals, there would be no events.

"I can help you out on that score if you'd let me."

Let him? Walker would beg him to if necessary. He pretended a casual air. "If you want to do that, I'm happy to let you."

"My pleasure." They shook hands. After some discussion about what they would need, Josie and Walker left and headed back to the manse.

Out of sight of the barn, Josie stopped, faced him, and began to laugh.

He stared, wondering what was so funny.

JOSIE STIFLED her amusement at the puzzled look on Walker's face. "We're quite the pair, aren't we? All eager to plan a rodeo and raise money but forgetting the most important thing." She grinned widely. "Some rodeo it would have been without the animals."

Walker pushed his hat back and wiped his forehead. "I'm sure one of us would have eventually realized that small oversight."

She chuckled. "Maybe, when it was too late to arrange it."

Walker laughed and drew her arm through his.

She left it there even though she knew she shouldn't. Lisa and Sylvie's comments made her realize how easily people would get the wrong idea about her and Walker.

Not any easier than she might if she wasn't careful.

"I told you I didn't know anything about planning an event," he said. He drew to a sudden stop and looked at her, his face wreathed in worry. "Is there anything else we've overlooked?"

She tipped her head and gave it serious consideration. "We can use the corrals at the west side of town. We have time, place, and fees. Sylvie is going to sell coffee. Can't think of anything else we need."

"Except a trick roper." His gaze went back to the barn. "If anyone knows where we might find one, I think it would be Mickey. Come on, let's ask him." He drew her after him back to the barn, where they posed the question to Mickey.

The man leaned back on his heels and grinned at them. "A kid still wet behind the ears was here a couple of weeks ago bragging about how good he was. I put it down to hot air, but then he showed me. I was impressed."

"What was his name, and do you have any idea where we might find him?"

"Only name he gave me was Roper. He said, 'My name is my skill.' Can't say if he made up the name or not. He said he was headed out to the Bar K looking for a job." Mickey came down hard on the soles of his feet. "Say, Earl Douglas will be in tomorrow to visit Sylvie. You could ask him about the kid."

"Thanks." Walker cheered as they turned down the street toward home. "It sounds like we might get us a trick roper."

Josie couldn't help but laugh at his excitement and feel a bit of pleasure that she could be part of his enjoyment.

They reached home. He ducked into the addition. "Guess I should get some work done." He was whistling as she went into the kitchen. She closed the door and leaned against it, still smiling.

Ma and Pa were absent, but Stella looked at her.

"You seem pleased with yourself. I'm guessing you had a pleasant morning." Stella's smile was warm as if she liked what she saw.

Josie laughed. "It was very successful. Norm will let me display my sewing at the store." She could hardly keep her feet to a normal pace as she crossed to the stove. "I'm going to make a fancy cowboy shirt and see if I can sell some when folks come for the rodeo."

"That's a good idea. When did you think of that?"

"It was something Walker said last night." Josie saw the way Stella's eyes brightened, and she hurried on before the woman could jump to any false conclusions. "We took the handbills to be distributed. We put up three posters. Sylvie said she would serve coffee and collect money from its sale to add to the proceeds. Mickey is going to arrange for stock and get this!" She couldn't keep her voice from revealing her pent-up joy and hoped Stella wouldn't mention it. She couldn't explain it to herself, let alone someone else. "Mickey knows someone who can do trick roping." Her smile was wide, and she guessed her eyes flashed with the happiness bursting from her heart.

She could not have denied that the morning of talking and laughing with Walker was somehow responsible.

"You know what's funny?" she continued. "We hadn't even considered the animals we'd need until Mickey asked about it."

Stella studied her with a sober expression. "As if God knew what you'd need and arranged for it?"

Josie blinked. She hadn't even considered that. And

her one of the preacher's daughters? "God is good and provides in surprising ways."

Stella looked troubled. "I wish I could see it happening in my life."

Josie's happiness made her want Stella to see that God had been working in her life and would continue to do so. "But didn't God send someone to rescue you when you were close to death? And didn't you end up here, where you are welcome and cared for?"

Stella nodded. "He did. Please understand that I'm grateful. It's just that I feel like my life is stalled. When my husband was alive, we had so many plans for the future. Now I have none. It's like the future has been snatched away from me."

Josie's heart went out to the woman who wasn't much older than herself. She sat by Stella and took her hands. Cold and trembling. "I'm sure God has something wonderful planned for you even if you can't see it at the moment." But if Josie's goal of having her own business and providing for her own future was taken away, she would feel every bit as defeated as Stella did. "Sometimes it's hard to trust when we can't see, but I suppose trust that has to see isn't really trust."

"I simply have no choice but to trust God for the future." Stella returned to her knitting.

Josie decided not to tell Stella that she herself wasn't fully convinced either. "Where's Ma and Pa?"

"They went over to the church. I believe they wanted to be alone."

"Where are the children?" It was strangely quiet.

"Jean took them. She'll bring them back when it's time for Blossom to have her nap."

It was nice that Stella had a friend who helped with the children.

Josie went to the stove. "I'll finish getting dinner ready." Ma had left a pot of soup simmering. Josie mixed up a pudding, sliced bread, and set the table.

She went to the door and called, "Dinner." Would Ma and Pa hear her? Or should she run over to the church? She didn't want to intrude, so she waited.

Walker came from the addition. "It's hard to believe the morning is already gone. I haven't achieved much here."

His words were a sharp reminder of how little time she had to get her sewing projects completed and ready to display.

Her parents came from the church. Good. No reason to delay dinner. She hurried inside, served the soup, and waited for the others to sit. No one seemed inclined to linger at the table. Her parents went back to the church as soon as the meal was over. Stella's children returned and she and Blossom went to their room. Donny asked to go back to Jean's and play with her children. He was given permission. Walker went out to the addition.

Josie climbed the stairs, sat at the window, and picked up the dress she was fashioning. This was her favorite spot to work. She could enjoy the view from the window. However, her gaze did not seek the trees along the river, nor the tidy rows of the garden—both things she normally enjoyed from her vantage point. No, instead, she watched Walker go to the stack of lumber, pick up a piece of wood, and hold it up as if measuring it with his eye. He set it aside and examined a second piece. It must have satisfied him, for he carried it into the building.

He was a careful man. She'd seen it in the way he did every task, whether coloring a poster or hanging a door.

A careful man would not understand the life Josie had once lived.

She ducked her head and resumed her project. Nothing mattered but getting this dress finished and making a shirt so she could get orders.

WALKER CONCENTRATED on building a cupboard for the workroom. It was time he finished up and moved on. Just as soon as he heard back from his uncle. Though how long would he wait before he had to go looking for him? He'd forget about his uncle but for his promise to his ma. And of course, there was the rodeo. He chuckled. The rodeo promised to be lots of fun.

He paused and looked toward the house. Hadn't he and Josie enjoyed a few laughs about forgetting that they needed animals? If only they hadn't forgotten anything else.

Like the fact Josie had no interest in a broke cowboy.

Determined to concentrate on the work before him, he measured, cut, and nailed pieces into place.

The house door opened, and his good intentions disappeared. He glanced that direction. Stella moving outside to sit in the sun.

Walker waited, but Josie did not join the woman.

He returned to his task. It wasn't like he expected she would. Or that he imagined she would saunter over and talk to him. Of course, he didn't. Neither of them was what the other needed.

He meant to keep moving.

She wasn't going anywhere. Didn't need anyone.

He made up his mind. By the time of the rodeo, he should be able to finish the work he'd told Jacob he'd do. He'd buy his tack and horse, pay his bill at the store, and move on.

CHAPTER 11

*T*he next morning Walker left the house as soon as breakfast was over. He'd noticed that Josie had brought her sewing down to the kitchen. She was obviously anxious to get her projects ready to display. Eager to live out her dream of independence. No need of anyone else.

He told himself it didn't matter. But he couldn't convince himself even though he reiterated the list he'd mentally made the night before.

He heard the door open and close and glanced up to see the elder Kinsleys go to the church. He watched until they were inside. Did they often go there to be alone? He smiled. It must be nice to need each other that much.

Donny raced past the addition and into the kitchen. He yelled, "Someone's comin'."

Walker remained where he was, out of sight but able to see what was going on.

A trail dusty cowboy approached the door. Josie stood in the narrow opening.

The cowboy doffed his hat, dismounted, and stood a few feet away. He held out a handbill. "I wanna enter this."

Walker decided it was time for him to make an appearance. "How can I help you?" he said.

The cowboy repeated his request.

"I'll get paper and pen and start a list." Josie hurried to the sitting room and returned with the items. Walker and the other man waited in the doorway.

Josie sat at the table. "Name? Event?" She wrote as the information was given.

"I got the money right here." He handed it to Walker.

The two men shook hands, and the cowboy left.

"What do I do with the money?" Walker asked. He hadn't given the entries and the entrance money any thought. Thankfully, Josie seemed to know what to do.

"I'll get a tin." She found a square one and handed it to him.

"I guess you better keep it here." He didn't want it out in the addition where anyone could come in and take it.

She put it on the middle shelf of the cupboard and closed the door. "It will be safe here."

"Fine." He went back to his work. But a few minutes later, Donny yelled.

"Another cowboy comin.'"

Again, Walker went out to greet the man and again, Josie wrote down his name and the events he wished to enter. Walker put the money in the tin and returned to his work.

But they both soon learned they wouldn't be getting a lot of work done that day. Again and again a cowboy or a pair of them, even a trio once, came to the door and were entered into the rodeo.

Dinner was interrupted by cowboys. The afternoon brought more of them.

Mrs. Kinsley and the preacher spent the morning in the church and then, after dinner, left to visit someone.

Stella went to her room for her usual afternoon sleep.

That left Josie basically alone with man after man coming to her door.

Walker stopped working in the addition where he was making cupboards. Instead, he did his best to look busy in the yard, his presence plainly visible to any visitors. He understood that they were likely all decent men. But he'd spent enough time working on ranches to know there were always one or two bad apples with no consideration for what was right or wrong.

Over supper, Jacob said, "Seems everyone wants to be part of this event."

"Sorry, sir. I didn't know it would be like this." Walker had to admit he hadn't known what to expect. If he had realized men would be riding into the yard all day, he probably wouldn't have thought the rodeo was such a good idea.

"No need to apologize," Jacob said. "It means the event will be successful."

Josie must have read the uncertainty in Walker's expression. "That's good. It's what we want."

"Yes, of course."

No one invited him to hang around after supper. Perhaps everyone was tired. He made his way to his room and stood by the window that allowed him a view of barn where the new horse grazed contentedly. Beyond that was the dusty street and the river. He angled his shoulder to the window frame. Tomorrow was Sunday. Perhaps he would ask Josie to walk with him by the river. They could go over the plans for the rodeo and make sure they hadn't forgotten anything else.

Darkness filled the corners and drifted across the room. It was time for bed. Tired from staying up late the night before to make posters, he was soon asleep.

AFTER SUNDAY BREAKFAST, Walker accompanied the family as they crossed to the church. They barely made it inside before folks started to arrive. Jonathan Bates was among the first. He hurried up the aisle to inquire after Jacob's health.

"I'm glad you're up to delivering the sermon," the old cowboy said. "It will do my soul good."

The married Kinsley sisters and their husbands arrived. Young Matt, the half-grown boy who lived with Eve and Cole, was with them, as were two older ladies— one in a wheelchair—who shared Eve and Cole's home. They were introduced as Cole's aunt and mother.

Everyone expressed their relief that the preacher looked so much better.

Jacob opened with prayer. Eve played the piano, and sitting by Walker, Josie sang sweetly.

Walker drank in every note of the music and every word of Jacob's sermon. A man could get used to being surrounded by caring, generous, loving people.

After the service many spoke to Walker about the rodeo. He was glad Josie stayed at his side to help answer the various questions. The crowd finally dispersed, and the family returned to the manse where they gathered round the table for dinner. Walker wasn't part of the family, but he was included.

The thought jarred through him. He hadn't felt part of a family since the Texas ranch was sold even though he'd had a ma and pa. He tried to think why that was so, but his attention was diverted by something Kade said to Flora, and he forgot the question.

The family was at times joking and laughing. At other times, they were serious and thoughtful. The elder Kinsleys, Cole's ma and aunt, and Mr. Bates went to the parlor to visit.

Stella and her children had, again, gone to see her friend.

The conversation around the table turned to plans for the rodeo, and Josie and Walker explained what they'd done.

Josie laughed, her teasing gaze catching Walker in its grasp as she told about Mickey asking about the stock. "Would you believe neither of us had considered getting animals?" Her grin widened. "It's understandable on my part, but Walker? And him being a cowboy. A Texas cowboy at that." She shook her head. "Sure beats me how he didn't think of it."

The others laughed, and Walker endured a few minutes of good-natured joshing. He didn't mind. In fact, it was more than worth it to see the way Josie smiled at him.

He decided to turn the tables. "You wouldn't believe the number of cowboys coming to the house yesterday. Seems they were only too glad of the excuse. Some of them looked like they would've paid for the pleasure of the visit. Never mind entering a rodeo."

That shifted the teasing to Josie.

"Any of them catch your eye?" Cole asked.

She shook her head. "All too dusty."

"Shall I send them back after they clean up?" Reese said.

"Not interested." Josie's reply was dismissive.

"Oh, you boys know Josie doesn't intend to marry." Flora flipped a red braid over her shoulder as she talked. "She thinks love is too great a risk."

The girls nodded, and the men stared at Josie.

"Isn't that right?" Flora persisted.

Josie darted a look at Walker then scowled at her sister. "I never said that." She sat up straighter and gave them all a look of disdain. "Though I might not deny it either."

Her comment earned her a burst of arguments.

Walker knew she meant to get a reaction from them, but he couldn't help but wonder how much truth was in her words. He meant to challenge them without being confrontational. "Maybe it isn't love that's the risk. After all, look at your parents."

"Can't," Josie said. "They've gone to the parlor."

Walker waved her comment away as the others waited for him to finish. "You all know that their love has endured through good times and bad."

They murmured agreement.

"So maybe it's something else."

"Such as?" Eve prompted.

"I can't say, because it's likely something different for everyone."

Those around him looked thoughtful.

"You might be right," Flora said. "For me it wasn't love I feared but loving and losing." She turned her adoring gaze to Kade. "I had to believe that love was worth whatever it cost." She looked at Kade. "I would gladly choose a few days of enjoyment with you over many days of loneliness."

Victoria leaned forward to get everyone's attention. "I suppose it was different for me too. I didn't know who I was because of my amnesia. That made me afraid of both my past and the future. I trusted Reese enough to know he would be there for me no matter what."

Walker turned to Eve wondering if she would explain what she had feared. What risk did love require of her?

She smiled around the table. "I had lost my parents and my brother. Even felt like I lost Flora when she married Kade. I was afraid of love. I was afraid of how easily it could be snatched away. I guess I was a bit like Flora in that sense. But Cole made me realize that love is the end of risks because only in love is my heart safe."

The girls all sighed.

Then they turned to Josie.

She held up her hands as if to ward off what they meant to say. "I'm quite happy with my life and plans."

Victoria smiled. "You are now, but some day you'll realize what you're missing."

Eve sighed. "Only in love is your heart safe."

"Listening to you girls is even more uplifting than going to church," Cole said, and everyone laughed, the atmosphere lightened.

They left the table and went outside. They explored

the addition and commented on the progress Walker had made.

"We had a few interruptions," he said by way of explaining why he hadn't done more. "First, we had to get the handbills made for the rodeo and then all those cowboys." He waggled his eyebrows and grinned at Josie.

"They did not come to see me," she insisted.

That brought hoots from the others.

They went to the corral so Flora could see the horse she had given to her father. "Walker," she said. "When do you want your horse?"

"What's his name?" He knew he sounded wary. Suspicious even.

Josie told about the horse named Sue, and everyone had a good chuckle.

"I wish you had warned me." Flora sounded so regretful that Walker knew the horse had a girlie name.

"Not Sue?"

"No, not Sue."

"Betty?" He shuddered at the thought.

"Nope." She leaned back on the corral fence and waited for him to guess.

"Mary? Martha?" He guessed six more names, and each time she said no.

Finally, he tossed his hands in the air. "I give up. Tell me. Put me out of my misery."

"Buck."

"Buck? That's a good name. Wait a minute. Why is he called Buck?"

Flora lifted a shoulder dismissively. "I'll let you find that out."

Kade pulled her to his side. "Stop tormenting the man. Buck's a good horse. You won't be disappointed."

Walker shrugged. "Whether or not he bucks, I will ride him."

Reese clapped him on the back. "Spoken like a true cowboy."

A TRUE COWBOY. The words echoed in the back of Josie's mind as she said good-bye to the others. True cowboys were homeless, restless. She had never seen herself happy in the roles her sisters had. But Eve's words dogged her every thought. *Only in love is your heart safe.* Josie would like to know that sort of assurance, but what the others didn't know was how damaging her secrets were. Love would require truth. Truth would destroy love. It was an impossible situation.

"Let's walk down by the river," Walker said. "We should maybe go over the plans for the rodeo in case we've missed anything."

She could hardly refuse him, so they crossed to the river. They turned away from town and walked in contemplative silence for a time. Her thoughts went over and over what her sisters had said. And for the first time ever, she admitted she wanted what they had.

But her past would not allow it.

"I like your sisters," Walker said, jarring her from her contemplation.

She chuckled. "I do too. We're a great bunch."

"Yup. I'd have to agree." He pulled her arm through

his. "Funny too. And maybe sometimes..." His voice deepened. "Infuriating."

She stopped, jerking him to a halt. "Infuriating? How so?"

"I'm only guessing here, but I wonder if those three girls didn't make their husbands work and worry before they married them."

Knowing he spoke of the others, she relaxed. "Of course, they did."

"Why do you say of course?"

"Because if a man loves a woman, he should be willing to prove it."

"How would a man prove it to you?"

His blue, probing look had the power to poke holes in her defenses.

"I suppose a man should be able to overlook flaws." She swallowed hard. "Forgive the unforgivable, bear the imperfections. See beyond facts to feelings and reasons." She forced herself to stop before she said more. Even so, she wondered if she'd said too much. Given him reason to have questions about her.

He drew his finger across her cheek and tucked a loose strand of hair behind her ear. "I'll keep that in mind."

His words were so soft. His touch so gentle that for a moment she couldn't think past either. Then he began walking, keeping her close to his side.

They reached a grassy spot where the river widened out.

"Shall we sit?" he asked.

She did not refuse even though her insides twitched at how easy it was to agree. She must be careful and not say more than she should. Or worse, let herself care for this man more than was safe.

He plucked a blade of grass and turned it over and over between his fingers. "I think this is the longest I've been without a horse since I was eight years old. That's when Pa and Uncle Paul gave me a real horse rather than a pony, and I went with them on the roundup." He grew thoughtful. "Ma said I was too young, but they both said it wasn't too early to begin learning the ins and outs of the ranch I would someday own."

Seeing the sadness in his face, Josie squeezed his arm, startled at the warmth that filled her at the touch. "I'm sorry things didn't work out."

He shrugged and pressed his hand over hers where it lay on his arm. "I suppose it will always hurt. But a man has to move on." He looked toward the horizon. "This country reminds me a lot of Texas."

"You sound surprised."

"Montana Territory doesn't look like Texas."

"Then how does it remind you of your former home?"

He was silent a moment. She could tell he was considering his reply. He faced her as he spoke. "It's you and your family. I see something there that I lost when the ranch was sold."

She tried to think what he meant. "I don't understand."

He gave a self-mocking chuckle. "I'm not sure I do either. But there's something about you and your family that makes me feel welcome. Makes me feel as if—" He stopped and shook his head.

She waited a second. "How does it make you feel?"

He searched her gaze, his look probing deep.

She let him, not knowing what he sought but certain he would not find it in her. Her heart must remain closed. And yet his gentle searching made the walls creak. Like the city of Jericho in the Bible, she thought with a touch of irony. If he blew a trumpet right now, the walls would crumble. She didn't mean a real trumpet, of course. In fact, she didn't know what she meant.

A slow, heart-stopping smile curved his lips. "It makes me feel like I want to belong, put down roots..." His voice trailed off as if he had said more than he meant.

Or perhaps was only discovering how he felt as he spoke.

Her insides quaked. Those words might have been the trumpet sound she feared. And longed for. The walls were about to crumble. Just in time, he chuckled and turned back to studying the landscape. She sucked in a strengthening breath, feeling as if she had jerked back from a frightening precipice.

"It's beautiful country. The mountains. The rolling grassy hills. An abundance of water. Great cattle country."

She gladly changed the subject. While she still had the will to do so. "I wasn't eager to move west. To me, Ohio was where I belonged. There were more people. More ladies willing to pay for my services as a seamstress. I know it will take more time and work to build up enough customers here."

"So, you regret the move?"

Her smile was from her heart. "Not at all. I have come to enjoy the mountains. They speak to me of strength and shelter. Like the Bible verse, 'As the mountains are round about Jerusalem, so the Lord is round about his people from henceforth even for ever.' What can be more reassuring than to know that God surrounds us with His love?"

"Your faith is strong."

She chuckled. "Pa and Ma have taught me the peace of putting my faith in God." She turned her head to study Walker. "How would you describe your faith?"

He rested his cheek on his drawn-up knee, his face very close to where their hands lay. If anyone watched them, she would have withdrawn her hand, but they were alone, and she saw no reason to break the contact and perhaps end the way they were opening up to each other.

"I might have lost my faith if not for my ma. She believed so deeply, even in her last months of pain. More than once, I railed against a God who would let her suffer like that. Every time I did, she would make me sit by her bed and listen to her. 'Should we only accept ease and comfort from God?' she'd say. 'Who is to say if the hard things we face are not what makes us into beautiful creations for God's glory?'"

"That's a lovely way of looking at it. I think your mother must have been one of those beautiful creations."

"She was. She often quoted a verse from Job. 'Though He slay me, yet will I trust in Him.' She said that was her goal." He seemed lost in his thoughts. "Not only did she make me promise to find Uncle Paul and talk to him, she made me promise to hold tight to my faith. She said I would no doubt encounter disappointments in my life, challenges beyond my ability to cope, but God would never fail to guide me."

Josie's throat tightened. "You have a wonderful heritage." The words sounded husky.

"I do, don't I?" He squeezed her hand. "So, do you."

"With the Kinsleys, yes." The walls around her heart cracked and shook. It was on the tip of her tongue to say her previous life had left her a heritage of shame and regret. But she could not let those words escape. She pulled her hand to her lap.

He slowly turned his face away, leaving her feeling bereft. However, when he didn't shift away or get to his feet, she pulled the comfort of his presence around her.

He pointed out the shape of the clouds and how the setting sun draped them in gold. They watched the banners of color fill the western sky. The draws in the distant mountains grew indigo in color.

"My ma always said God delights in filling the world with beauty," he said, his tone reverent.

"My ma used to say that when the sun sets, chickens know enough to go to roost, and people should know enough to go to bed." Josie chuckled. "Of course, she only said that when we girls didn't want to settle down at night."

Walker laughed and got to his feet. He held out a hand to help her up. "We better go back before she has reason to scold us for being dumber than chickens."

He held her hand as they returned home, and she let him, even though a corner of her heart, behind her protective walls, reminded her that if she let herself grow too fond of this cowboy, she wouldn't be able to keep her secrets locked away.

She pulled her hand from his, hoping he would think

it was because they had reached the house. "Good night," she said.

"Good night. Sleep well." He waited at the doorway until she stepped inside.

Not until she had retired to bed, did she realize they had not once talked about the rodeo.

They'd have to do that tomorrow.

She ignored the way her heartbeat picked up pace at the idea of another evening spent in Walker's company. The next time she would make sure they restricted the conversation to rodeo plans, and she would keep her hands locked together at her waist.

CHAPTER 12

*W*alker lay on his cot, his hands behind his head as he went over the day. Like he'd told Josie, he enjoyed her family. And more…a sense of home. He grinned. No doubt his enjoyment had something to do with the many hours he spent in Josie's company. Although she held back as if not willing to trust him, she also reached out to him. Her hand had offered comfort and something more, though he wasn't prepared to say what that was.

For now, he was content to spend as much time with her as possible and learn as much as he could.

Over the next few days, they fell into a pattern. He worked on the cupboards and shelves in the addition. Josie kept busy with helping with housework, laundry, and the gardening.

"The beans are coming on," she told him, and he watched as she, her mother, and Stella picked bushels of them and then steamed up the inside of the house canning them.

At the end of their work, Josie wiped her brow and looked at the many jars cooling on the cupboard. "It always pleasures me to see the cellar shelves fill up with winter supplies."

In the evenings, despite how hard she'd worked all day, she sat outside and sewed. He'd hoped they could walk along the river again, but she was too busy.

One evening she finished the dress and held it up for him to look at.

He didn't know much about ladies' garments, but the dress looked good and he said so.

"I'm trying to decide what color to make the cowboy shirt," she said.

Walker sat down beside her. "For fancy shirts, it seems to me the cowboys like something bright. Red or blue."

Josie had paper and pencil and sketched out an idea for a shirt. "What do you think of this?"

He examined the drawing. "I've seen them with bigger yokes and shiny buttons holding the yokes in place."

She returned her attention to the paper and sketched a few lines then handed it back to him. The yoke went almost to the waist and big buttons adorned it. She giggled, and he understood she meant to tease him.

"This is great."

"Really? Rather peacockish, isn't it?"

"Young cowboys are usually peacockish."

They both laughed.

"Of course, you could offer to make each shirt to order, so no young peacock would have a shirt like another young peacock."

"Good idea." She returned to the paper. Soon she had sketches of a dozen shirts. The yokes varied in size and shape. For some she had made the yoke patterned. She handed the paper to him and waited for his approval.

He nodded. "You're rather good at this. I think you won't need rich, fancy-dressed women. You'll get all the business you need from fancy-dressed cowboys."

"If I do it is thanks to your help."

The next few days he watched her cut out a shirt in a bright blue color.

"Some cowboy is going to think he's pretty special in that shirt," he said as she sat outside sewing the seams.

"There haven't been many cowboys coming by to sign up for the rodeo lately."

Only four had been by during the week. "Wait until Saturday."

His prediction was right. On Saturday, a steady stream of men came to the door to pay to enter events.

And then it was Sunday again. Josie would not be sewing today or picking beans. Though she would likely be visiting with her family.

But neither Eve nor Victoria and their husbands came to church.

"Sometimes there are reasons they can't be away so long," Josie said.

Flora and Kade were there but hurried away as soon as they'd eaten dinner, saying they'd seen signs of coyotes hanging about and didn't want to leave the place for long.

Walker and Josie were alone. "Shall we walk?" he asked.

"I suppose we need to go over plans for the rodeo. I

can't believe it is only a few days away. Do we have everything in order?"

"Let's check on the corrals." Side by side, they made their way to the edge of town where sturdy corrals had been previously built near the railway tracks. There were three pens. "Perfect. The stock can go into those two pens. The events can take place in this one. There's plenty of room for people to sit and watch. Someone has even built some benches." Three rows of them were on one side of the corrals. He was excited for the day. A rodeo was always great entertainment. But he was also sad. After this, he would have no reason to stay. He didn't know which emotion was strongest. Before he could decide, young Jimmy raced to them.

"Mickey and me built those benches. Don'cha think that's a good idea?"

"It's a great idea," Walker said.

"I can hardly wait for next Saturday." The boy rocked back and forth. "It's all anybody talks about. Ma says we are going to get lots of books from the money raised. She says boys and girls and grownups too, need books. Says it helps us be better ed'cated."

Jimmy climbed the fence and studied the inside of the pen. "Sure hope it don't rain." He jumped down and trotted off.

"Rain?" Josie's face wrinkled with worry. "What will we do if it does?"

"I don't know. I guess we'll cross that bridge when we get to it."

She snorted. "A bridge, you say. How much rain are you anticipating?"

He chuckled at the way her eyes sparkled as she

turned his saying into a dire prediction. "We could always change to water events."

She laughed. "Instead, let's pray for good weather."

He pulled her arm through his. "In the meantime, let's enjoy the sunshine."

They meandered down the street and eventually reached the river. A bench sat on the bank, practically begging them to sit there. They didn't argue with the invitation.

In the hours they'd spent together over the past week, Walker had grown more and more comfortable in her presence. He felt safe enough that he'd told her about different events on the Texas ranch.

"Tell me what you did while you were living in town with your mother," she said after they'd discussed the view from where they sat. "Who did you spend time with? I'm assuming you didn't spend it all with your mother."

"No, she wouldn't allow it. Said I should be with people my own age."

Josie darted a look at him out of the corner of her eyes. "Did that include young women your own age?"

He tucked a smile into her heart at the way she pretended to be only casually interested. "There was a mix of both ladies and gents."

"Hmm."

He knew what she wanted to know, but he'd make her ask.

"No special young woman?"

He grinned, pleased she cared. "I told you about Dianne. She wanted to settle down. She constantly talked about having a big house. She begged me to go into partnership with her brother. I didn't much care for that. Her brother was overbearing. Didn't care who he hurt in making a dollar."

He'd told Josie much of this already but found he wanted to give her more details.

"When her brother found another partner, Dianne switched loyalties really fast. Said the new guy—Denton —was far more ambitious than I was. More what she wanted in a man. My mother was dying, so I couldn't leave town. But I sure did my best to avoid Dianne. She tracked me down once several months later and said she'd made a mistake. Denton wasn't what she hoped for. She begged me to take her back. But she'd already made it clear that I wasn't what she wanted either, and I told her so. I said I hadn't changed, and I didn't expect she had. I made sure to avoid her after that even if I had to be rude."

"That must have been painful."

"It was at the time." He let the words hang there, wanting her to ask more. Wanting her to care.

* * *

JOSIE KEPT her attention on the trunk of a nearby tree. Of course, he'd had lady friends. Likely lots of them, but she didn't want to hear about them. And to think that a young woman had broken his heart...well, maybe it helped explain why he didn't want to settle down.

"At the time?" She wondered what he meant.

"It always hurts to be rejected, but it didn't take long for me to realize her feelings were fickle, and I was fortu-

162

nate to discover it. I realize now it was my pride that was hurt more than my heart."

The way he looked at her made her eyes sting. Was he offering her something? His heart?

She turned back to the tree and kept her gaze glued to it.

"What about you?" he asked. "How many young men have broken their hearts over you?"

"None."

"No beaus? I find that hard to believe."

He wouldn't if he knew how she deflected any male attention. "Maybe once, if you count Percy Condor. I was persuaded to go with him to a social event. He called on me a few times after that."

"What happened?"

"Nothing. I just couldn't imagine him in my life."

"That's right. Josie said you think love is too great a risk." He crossed his arms and for a moment seemed dismayed by her attitude then he gave her hard study. "What is it you fear?"

The truth. She feared people learning the truth. But she could not say that. She held his gaze without faltering as she answered. "The only thing I fear is being without a home."

Their gazes locked, went on and on. He would never understand what her childhood was like, and she would never tell him.

"Someday," he murmured. "You'll tell me why."

She scrambled to her feet. "It's time for me to go."

He fell in at her side, lengthening his stride as she rushed homeward. Realizing she could not outdistance him, she forced herself to slow down and act as if nothing was wrong.

She ached to tell him. But it was too great a risk.

* * *

THE NEXT FEW days passed quickly. She finished the shirt. Walker declared it was the nicest shirt he'd ever seen, and he went with her to display both the shirt and her finished dress in the store. He had even helped her design a poster advertising her sewing business and made certain she mentioned that each cowboy shirt would be different.

Pa was feeling well enough that he rode his horse and made calls on those who needed his attention.

Ma sang as she worked, happy to see Pa doing better.

Even Stella was getting stronger.

Josie was grateful for all the improvements, but they made her feel less and less needed. She consoled herself with the hope of soon having her own source of income and her own place to live.

Josie had promised herself she would avoid spending time with Walker. Being with him threatened the walls around her heart, and that frightened her as much as meeting a gunman with his gun aimed at her chest. But she found it was easier to plan to avoid him than to actually do it.

Once the sewing projects were done, they walked along the river in the evening. She allowed herself several reasons for sharing the evening hours with him.

They needed to review the rodeo. They never did.

She wanted to pray with him for good weather. That

only took two minutes of the hour or two of time together.

She needed his advice on designing shirts.

Even she didn't believe that one.

* * *

SATURDAY FINALLY ARRIVED. The day of the rodeo. They went to the corrals early in the morning. Animals milled about, mooing and neighing. Mickey gave instructions to a dozen cowboys on horseback.

"They're in charge of bringing out the animals as they're needed," Walker said.

Two hours before time to start, the place was crowded with wagons and horses. People packed the benches and the grassy area. Sylvie's coffee sold as fast as she could make it.

Mickey had offered—maybe even begged—to be the announcer and entered the corral with a megaphone. He soon had everyone's attention.

"Let's find a place to sit," Walker said.

Josie had seen her family on the far side of the corrals, but Walker didn't make any attempt to reach them. They found a spot where they could sit side by side if they crowded close together. She told herself it was okay because they didn't have a choice. But she secretly rejoiced at it.

The first event was team roping, and Josie watched in admiration at the skill of these cowboys. Steer wrestling followed. She marveled at the brute force needed for a man to throw a big steer to the ground. She knew it couldn't be as easy as they made it look.

The wild horse riding was next.

She shuddered at the way the men were tossed about in the saddle. Most of them ended up in the dirt, but each got up and waved his hat to the crowd and was cheered for his effort.

Mickey introduced Roper, and Josie had to agree that the young man was very skilled. He twirled the rope over his head and close to the ground. He made a huge loop parallel to his body and skipped through it. He swung two loops at once, and if that wasn't hard enough, he jumped in and out of the two loops going at the same time.

"I'm impressed," she whispered to Walker.

"Me too," he whispered back, his breath warm of her cheek.

She sighed with contentment. She had nothing to do but sit back and enjoy the day. And the pressure of Walker's arm against hers.

"I think you'll like the wild cow milking," he said.

He was right.

She laughed and cheered at the scramble of cowboys and cows. By the time one team had successfully gotten a few squirts of milk into the pail, she was wiping her eyes.

The cows were chased from the corral. Mickey announced the horse races would begin. The crowd moved toward the roadway where the race was to start.

Walker pulled Josie to her feet.

There was a commotion behind them. Someone screamed. Walker and Josie turned to see what the cause was. Before she could make it out, Walker raced away, pushing through those around them.

Curious, Josie went to the fence where she could see.

She gasped. Her heart thudded against her ribs. Her breath stopped halfway down and would go no further. A steer raced toward the crowd, its eyes wide with fright, spittle flying from its mouth. A young family—a mother and two children—were directly in its path. Men waved their arms at the animal, but it charged onward. Why didn't the mother get up and drag her children to safety? But she didn't move.

And then Josie saw Walker. And everything slowed down. He ran directly toward the animal, jumping over objects in his path. She watched his feet clear a basket. Dust billowed up when his boots hit the ground. His feet lifted again. Both feet were off the ground at the same time as he rushed onward, closing the distance in strides that ate up the air. She saw his legs pump. The muscles in them flexed with the effort.

He reached the steer and grabbed for the horns. Long white horns with sharp tips. Their span was almost more than a man could reach. He caught the nearest horn, but the animal lowered his head and tipped his spear-like horns toward Walker. The animal's intent was plain to see. He meant to gore Walker.

Walker stayed upright. The strain showing in the way the fabric of his shirt stretched across his back. Again, he reached for the far horn. The steer swung his head. Walker's feet went one way as he went another. Somehow, he managed to keep his balance.

The steer continued to try and snag Walker with its horn.

Josie couldn't bear to watch as she imagined him falling under those pounding hooves and being trampled, his insides ripped open by those horns. But she couldn't look away. Silently she breathed a prayer. *God help him.*

One of Walker's hands touched the ground, and he righted himself. His feet fought for traction. He stretched, his arms wide. He managed to get hold of both horns and hung on as the steer lifted its head. Walker's feet barely remained on the ground. He threw himself away from the animal, using his weight to try and twist the animal's head and force it to stop. Instead, he was dragged, his heels digging uselessly into the grass.

Bits of dirt flew from his boots.

Someone had snatched the woman and children to safety.

Now Walker was the one in danger as the animal roared and fought Walker's grasp.

Help him, Josie tried to call, but her voice refused to work. Why wasn't someone rushing in to help?

The steer swung his head. Walker dug in his heels and wrenched the horns. The steer changed direction. Walker pulled again, pushing his weight into the turn. He kept twisting. The steer went down, Walker clinging to the massive horns. Half a dozen cowboys rushed in, roped the animal, and took it back to the pen with the others.

Walker lay on the ground, not moving.

Josie rushed forward but was blocked by dozens of others. She couldn't see him. She couldn't get to him.

She wouldn't cry.

A cheer went up. The crowed parted, and Walker limped toward her.

She grabbed the rail of the fence for support as her legs turned to water.

He slapped his hat against his leg, raising a puff of dust. His clothes were soiled. But he was whole.

She squinted to clear her vision and studied him. But she saw no sign of blood. The fact did not reassure her. He could have internal injuries.

He reached her side. "Shall we go see the races? Maybe Flora will win."

She couldn't move. Couldn't speak. Wasn't sure she even breathed.

He leaned closer, squinting. "Are you okay?"

"Okay?" The word squeezed past her clenched teeth. "I saw you almost killed. I'm not okay."

"I'm fine." He stayed close, his gaze watchful. "You aren't going to collapse, are you?"

"That was too close for comfort." If there hadn't been a crowd around them, any number of which would gladly report a lapse in proper conduct to her parents or anyone else who cared to listen, Josie would have wrapped her arms about Walker and held on to him until she stopped shaking. Instead, she mustered every bit of strength she could and straightened.

"Somebody had to stop the critter before someone got hurt." Walker made it sound like it was the most reasonable thing in the world to tackle a raging animal who was many times heavier than he.

In Josie's mind it was anything but normal.

A man took Walker's hand and shook it vigorously. "You saved my wife and children. Thank you."

Several others came up to him and shook his hand or slapped him on the back. Some called him brave. Some called him a hero.

Josie couldn't see it that way.

Walker pulled her to his side, and they made their way to the road where the contestants were lining up for the horse race.

By the time they found a place to watch, Josie had stopped shaking and began to hear what the others were saying. Slowly her fear changed to admiration for what Walker had done. He'd seen the danger and sprang into action before anyone else could think what to do. He'd taken a risk, but through it all, she had to admit he seemed to know what he was doing.

She knew an incredible sense of pride.

She leaned close to whisper, "That was the bravest thing I ever saw."

He looked surprised and then pleased. "I just did what needed to be done."

She smiled up at him, letting him know he had impressed her.

CHAPTER 13

She thought he was brave! Walker held the thought to him. He could have said it wasn't bravery. He simply knew what needed to be done and how to do it. Not once had he considered there to be any risk to himself. But there wasn't a chance to tell her as they watched the horse racing, cheering for Flora, who came in second to a spunky young cowboy.

The rodeo was over, but no one seemed anxious to end the day. Groups gathered round and visited as they shared the lunches they'd brought.

Sylvie spied Walker and Josie and hustled over with a tin full of money. "Did pretty good if I do say so myself."

Norm jogged over with another tin heavy with coins. He'd been in charge of taking admission. "I would say the day was successful in every way." He handed the money to Walker.

"What are your plans for the evening?" Sylvie asked.

"We have to take the money home," Josie said.

The elder Kinsleys had already left, and Josie's sisters visited with friends.

Sylvie got a gleam in her eyes. "I think you two deserve a treat for all your hard work. Tell you what. I'll prepare a picnic lunch for you to share."

Mickey had joined the conversation. "Good idea. I'll lend you a buggy. You two go enjoy having done such a good job."

Walker was about to protest that everyone had had a part in the event when Josie said, "I don't know. I really should get home."

At that, Walker changed his mind about refusing the offer. "We accept." He turned to Josie. "You deserve a little enjoyment."

She raised her eyebrows. "I just had an afternoon of enjoyment."

"Let's make the day complete then. And, at the same time, please Miss Sylvie and Mickey."

"You do know how to convince a girl." She turned to the others. "Very well. We accept your offer and thank you."

They made their way back to the manse. The journey took longer than usual as people wanted to talk to them, to thank them for the rodeo. Many thanked Walker for stopping the steer.

At the house, Josie put both cans of money in the cupboard with the square one holding the entrance money. "We'll count it later," she said. "Ma, Pa, Sylvie has prepared a picnic for us, and Mickey has lent us a buggy. We'll go for a drive if that's okay with you?"

Both parents waved them away. "Enjoy the rest of day."

Walker and Josie sauntered back to Main Street and picked up the picnic basket from Sylvie then made their way to the livery barn where Mickey had a horse and buggy ready to go.

"I feel like royalty at the way they treat us," Josie said as they drove away from town.

Walker stopped the buggy and jumped down. He plucked some spindly yellow flowers and twisted them together then climbed back to the wagon. "Lean over," he said.

"Why?"

"Just do it." He waited to see if she trusted him enough to obey without knowing why. His heart expanded three times when she did. He wrapped the rope of flowers around her head.

"I hereby crown you queen for the day."

She grinned. "What an honor." He was about to drive on when she said, "Stop." She climbed down and picked some long blades of grass and wove a bit of rope then stuck in three flowers. She got back up.

"Lean over." Their eyes locked together. Did she mean to ask him to trust her? He bent his head. She fiddled with his hat. "There. You are the conquering hero."

He lifted his hat from his head to see that she had wrapped the green and yellow rope around the brim. He replaced his hat and grinned at her as they drove onward.

"Where shall we go?" He didn't know the country well enough to choose a spot.

"There's a nice little hill a mile down the road."

"Then we'll go there." A few minutes later they reached the place she meant, and he helped her down. He half considered pulling her into his arms, but she stepped aside and pointed. "We can sit there to eat."

He lifted out the picnic basket and saw that Mickey had put in a blanket. He spread it for them to sit on.

As they munched on thick roast beef sandwiches, they went over the events of the afternoon.

"I was scared"—she looked down—"when I thought you were hurt."

He caught her chin and lifted her head, waited for her to meet his eyes. "I didn't mean to frighten you."

Her gaze dipped deep into his thoughts. He wanted nothing more than to assure her he would never hurt her. He lowered his head and kissed her gently even though he yearned to deepen the kiss, hold her to his heart, promise her…

She sat back, her head turned down.

"I'm not going to say I'm sorry," he said, brushing the back of his hand across her cheek. "Because I'm not. I've found something here, with your family…with you…that I've been looking for since the ranch sold."

She watched him, her expression full of longing.

He continued. "I've found a sense of belonging, of home, of security. I can see myself settling down in this area. Do you—"

She pressed her fingertips to his mouth. "Please don't say anything more."

"Why not? I want to tell you how I feel."

"There are things about me you don't know. Things that might change your mind."

He cupped his hand to the back of her neck. "Nothing could do that. I know your past was troubling, upsetting. But your past doesn't matter to me. All that matters is who you are now." He saw words building in her and hurried on before she could voice them. "I know you need to feel secure. I'll buy some land and build a house."

She shook her head. "I have never wanted to tell anyone the truth about who I am. What I am. But before you start making plans, you need to know everything."

"It won't matter." He was sure of his growing affection for her. Knew it could be called something deeper, more lasting. There was nothing she could say or do to change that. "The truth can't hurt anyone."

"Don't be so certain." She sat up straight, her hands knotted together in her lap. "I told you my uncle raised me. He didn't have gainful employment, so I never knew if we would have to leave in the middle of the night. I learned to sleep with my coat and shoes close by. I could not lose my coat, because inside the pocket, deep in a corner where it wouldn't get lost, was a thimble that had belonged to my mother. It was the only thing I had of hers."

Walker wanted to reach for her, cover her hands with his, pull her into his arms, but he sensed her memories made her fragile.

"I promised myself that when I grew up, I would never be without a home. One that was mine. One that I couldn't be chased from."

"I can promise you that."

She shuddered. "There's more." She turned at the sound of approaching horses. "Flora and Kade. What do they want?"

The pair rode toward them. Kade called to them. "We're on our way home but wanted to deliver a message. There's a man at the house asking after you, Walker."

"Did he give his name?"

"No, but he said it was of utmost urgency that he speak to you. I suggest you return to town."

Walker hesitated. He wanted to hear what Josie had been about to say. But Josie was already gathering up the picnic things.

They waved good-bye to Kade and Flora and drove back to town.

Josie didn't say anything, but the look of relief on her face made him understand she was glad to have been interrupted.

"We'll finish this conversation later," he said.

She nodded but kept her gaze averted.

What could she possibly have to say that was so bad in her eyes? Maybe that was the answer. She'd been a child, and whatever she had to confess was something that seemed awful to a child.

Relieved to have figured that out, he turned his attention to who might want to speak to him. Was someone unhappy with how the rodeo had been conducted? If so, he would do what he could to soothe the ruffled feathers.

They delivered the buggy to Mickey. They took the basket to Sylvie, thanked her for her kindness, then walked to the manse. A horse was tied at the corrals. A fine-looking horse. He might like to own a horse that looked that good.

Whoever wanted to see him must be waiting inside, so he and Josie went to the house.

He opened the door and stared at the man sitting at

the table visiting with the Kinsleys. He hadn't seen the man in twelve years, but he recognized him immediately.

"Uncle Paul."

* * *

MA AND PA introduced Mr. Jones to Josie. They didn't need to add that he was Walker's uncle. Walker had already informed everyone of that fact.

Josie stared at the man. She saw a family resemblance in the blue eyes and the shape of their faces. She looked from Walker to his uncle. They wore matching expressions of caution.

The man rose to his feet. A tall, lean man. He had a thick head of brown hair that contained silvery strands. No doubt Walker would look much like him when he aged.

He took a step toward Walker then hesitated. "I came as soon as I got your letter."

"I didn't expect you to."

Josie heard the strain in his words.

"I have always hoped I would get a chance to talk to you…explain…"

Ma and Pa rose. They signaled Josie to follow them from the room.

Walker's uncle held up his hand. "We'll go over to the corral to talk." He went to the door and waited.

Walker stood as if rooted to the floor.

His uncle's voice was gentle, pleading. "This is something you might want to hear on your own."

Walker slipped through the door. His uncle followed as they crossed to where the horse stood.

Josie went to the window to watch.

"Let them have their privacy," Pa said.

"I can't hear them." She moved away, pretending to be busy with something at the cupboard where she could still see them. "Walker was sure surprised to see his uncle."

Ma agreed. "Mr. Jones says he hasn't seen Walker or talked to him for twelve years. That's a long time for family to be apart. I hope they are able to resolve whatever it was that went wrong."

"Me too." But she knew family wasn't always a blessing.

As she watched, Walker recoiled as if struck, but his uncle had not lifted a hand. Rather, he held his palms upward in a placating way.

Walker shook his head.

His uncle nodded slowly then mounted his horse and rode down the back road toward Main Street.

Walker didn't move. His posture made her shudder. She'd expected seeing his uncle and talking to him would have been a happy moment. The way his shoulders were drawn up and his hands curled into fists said it hadn't

She waited, willing him to relax. When he didn't, she went to the door. "His uncle is gone. I'm going to talk to him." She closed the door before her parents could protest.

Walker didn't look at her, didn't even seem to be aware of her as she reached his side.

"Walker." She spoke his name softly.

He shuddered.

"Are you all right?"

A play of emotions crossed his face. Shock. Surprise.

Anger. "I don't know what I am. I don't even know who I am."

"That's a strange thing to say. You're Walker Jones, aren't you?" Wasn't he? Would it matter if he wasn't? Not in the least. She didn't care if he was Walker Jones or John Brown.

Walker looked at Pa's horse. "If I had a horse right now, I would gallop away until we both collapsed from exhaustion."

"Then perhaps it's a good thing you don't have one. Do you mind telling me what's wrong?" Tension tightened the muscles in her neck. This was the man to whom she had almost confessed her most fearful secrets. And she hardly recognized him.

He grabbed her hand. "If I can't ride, I'll have to walk."

Main Street was still busy with those who had come for the rodeo and stayed to enjoy the rest of the day. They crossed to the river. A family had a blanket spread out and were enjoying a picnic. They called out a greeting, but Walker rushed on.

Josie waved as they passed.

Two more families sat along the bank. Walker hurried onward as if he hadn't even seen them. He kept up a pace that had her trotting.

It had been several minutes since they had encountered anyone, and Josie was getting out of breath. She tugged on his hand. "Walker, slow down."

He ground to a halt and looked around as if only now realizing where he was. "Sorry. Let's sit."

They sat on the grassy bank. The water murmured past. Ducks quacked a protest at their intrusion. The setting was peaceful. The two people on the bank were not.

Josie waited, not wanting to push Walker. If he needed to talk, she was ready to listen. If he didn't want to talk....

Well, she would be patient.

"My uncle says he has a big ranch near Bella Creek. He has a big house."

"That's nice." Though she couldn't imagine why that would upset anyone.

"Nice for who?" He sucked in air. "He told me why he left and why the ranch was sold."

"I take it you didn't like the reasons."

Walker kept his gaze on the water gurgling over the rocks. "He said he's my father."

She jolted. "Your uncle is your father?"

Walker began slowly. "Seems my mother and my uncle had a—what did he call it?—an 'indiscretion' twenty-five years ago, and I was the result." Bitterness edged his words.

"My parents were married at the time. Adultery is what it was." Each word was spit out like it had soured in his mouth.

"I don't understand."

"You don't understand how my uncle and my mother could have—" He stopped. Swallowed hard. Shook his head. "Neither do I."

"What did your father think?"

"He didn't know. He thought I was his son, just as I did."

"Your poor mother. How difficult it must have been for her to keep that secret?"

"He—" He jabbed his thumb toward the house to indicate he meant his uncle. "Wanted to tell me when I turned twelve. That would mean telling my father. My mother begged him not to. Said it would do more harm than good. They argued. She made him promise to keep their secret."

"I'm guessing that's when he left."

"He said he couldn't live with the lie." He grabbed a rock near his foot and threw it into the river so hard that water splashed up on them. "But it was all right for them to let me live with a lie. He's my father. Some father. He couldn't even tell me the truth."

She didn't say anything, understanding that his world had been shattered.

He pounded out the words. "If they'd just told me the truth."

Hadn't he, only a few hours ago, said the truth couldn't hurt you? She wondered if he would say it now. "Maybe they were right not to tell you. You know the truth now, and you aren't handling it very well." She was so glad she hadn't told him her secrets. Was this how he would have reacted? Anger? Blame?

He turned away. "I thought you'd understand."

"I understand you're hurt. You're upset. Not sure who you are now. But Walker, how does any of this change who you are or what you want?"

Would he realize how important his answer was to her?

Walker stared at the water. "My uncle—How can I ever think of him as my father?—says he's always hoped I'd show up. He built a big house and a big ranch that he hoped to share with me some day. He wants me to become his partner."

Josie touched his arm, the coldness of his skin matching the coldness aching in her bones. Was he going to leave? Had he forgotten his promise to give her a home? When would she stop hoping it would be possible? "Is that what you want?"

He closed his eyes. "I don't know what to think. I don't know who I am." He jerked to his feet and pulled her up. "I need to think." They returned to the house, their steps every bit as hurried as the outward journey had been.

He released her hand before they stepped into the kitchen. Her parents still sat at the table, a Bible open between them.

"Mr. Kinsley, may I borrow your horse for a couple of hours? I want to ride out and get the horse Flora has for me."

"Of course, you may."

Walker twisted his hat between his white-knuckled fingers. "Could I ask for my wages? I need to pay for the horse and buy a saddle."

"Of course." Pa left the room and returned in a few minutes with some money. "I hope this will be enough for you."

Walker barely looked at the bills before he stuffed them into his shirt. "I'm sorry I didn't finish the job."

With every word, Josie's heart dipped toward the soles of her feet.

He strode from the house, and she followed. As he saddled Pa's horse, she managed to put her fear into words. "Walker, are you leaving?"

"I need time to think." He paused as he prepared to get into the saddle. "I need to figure this out."

For a moment, he looked like he might say something more, then he blinked. He might as well have pulled a thick wooden door over his thoughts with that simple flicker of his eyelids. He had closed himself off from her.

He rode from the yard in the direction of Flora and Kade's place.

Josie watched him long after he was out of sight.

With leaden feet, she made her way back to the house.

She still had her plans and her dreams. They had to be enough.

CHAPTER 14

Somehow Josie made it to her room without revealing her disappointment and crawled into bed. She slept fitfully, jerking awake to the sound of hoofbeats. She listened. Nothing. Only her wishful imagination. She woke three more times to silence except for the pounding of her heart.

The next morning, she hurried downstairs and glanced toward the corrals. No horses. He hadn't come back, not even to return Pa's horse. No doubt Flora and Kade would bring it when they came for church.

Church. She dreaded sitting alone on the pew, missing Walker beside her. Even more, missing him. But she would not plead illness. Instead, she made breakfast, laughed with the children, smiled at Stella and her parents.

She again heard hoofbeats but knew better than to think it was more than her imagination. But the sound grew louder.

"Someone coming," Pa said, and went to the window.

"It's Walker's uncle." He opened the door. "Join us for breakfast. There's plenty."

Mr. Jones glanced past Pa. "Is Walker here? I'd like to speak to him."

Pa shook his head. "He's gone."

A look of pain crossed the man's face. Much the same as the look Josie had seen on Walker's face. "Did he say where he was going?"

"Not to me," Pa said, and turned. "Josie?"

"He didn't say anything to me."

"Then I'll be headed back to the ranch. If you happen to see him, please tell him I am anxious to hear from him."

Pa watched as the man returned to his horse. "There goes a man who looks like the world has fallen down around him. Josie, what happened?"

She looked about the table. "It's not my story to tell." But she ached to share the news with her parents. She waited until the meal was over and the dishes done, knowing her parents would make a stop in their bedroom before going to church. She followed them.

"May I speak with you?"

"By all means." Pa led them to the parlor and closed the door.

She told them what Walker had told her.

Ma closed her eyes. "That poor boy. That poor man."

"We must pray for healing for them both." Pa bowed his head and prayed.

Josie expected it would only be about Walker and his uncle, but Pa added, "Help Josie also find healing and release from her past. For Your honor and glory. Amen."

"Pa, I'm fine." She gave her bravest smile.

He patted her shoulder. "Sometimes the past is hard to be shed of." He took a step toward the door.

"Wait," she said. "I don't know how much I should say to others."

"As you said, it's not your story to tell."

"What about my sisters?" They were the only ones she was thinking of.

Pa looked thoughtful. "We've never been a family to keep secrets." His words smote her.

He continued. "I think we should be honest with them and ask them to pray. Your sisters can be trusted not to gossip."

"Thank you." She filled her lungs. "I wasn't looking forward to having to carry such a big secret." There wasn't room inside for more.

A few minutes later, she went to church with them.

Victoria and Eve stared at the empty spot beside Josie.

"Where is he?" they asked.

Thankfully, Flora could answer. "He came and got his horse last evening. Said he had things to deal with and rode to the west." She gave Josie a sympathetic glance. "He had the look of a man who wanted to ride deep into the mountains and get lost. I'm so sorry, Josie."

Josie hoped her smile looked more real than it felt. "I always knew he would leave. He never made a secret of it. Just as I've never made a secret of my plans to have my own business."

She was grateful the service began then, making more conversation impossible. The music sounded flat in her ears, and Pa's words echoed so badly inside her head, she couldn't understand them.

Several people came up to her and asked about Walker's absence. When she said he had left to take care of another matter, they looked surprised and disappointed, then someone asked how much money had been raised.

With a start, she realized she'd forgotten about the fund raiser.

Pa overheard the question and came to her rescue. "The school board will get together tomorrow and count it. We'll decide then how to choose what books to order."

Her sisters and their husbands joined them for dinner after church. Cole's aunt and mother had not come, and Matt had stayed with them.

Stella had taken the children and gone to visit her friend.

As Josie helped serve the meal, she put off the many questions her sisters asked. She ignored the way their curious gazes went to the chair Walker would have normally occupied. She waited until they had all started to eat then put her fork down.

"Pa, should I tell them?"

"You're the one who heard it firsthand."

She looked down at her plate, drew in a calming breath, and looked across the table at Eve. "Walker's uncle is his father." She would have chuckled at their reaction except it hurt too much to try.

As soon as they settled down, she told them everything, including how surprised Walker was. "And upset."

Flora, the adventuresome one, said, "I knew he was looking like a man who needed to get away. He'll spend the winter in the mountains. Best thing for him."

Josie knew Flora didn't mean to hurt her, but the words gouged out a bleeding trail in her heart. The winter? A man who needed to get away?

"Then what?" Eve asked.

Flora shrugged. "Maybe he'll join his uncle—whoops, father—on a big ranch. Sounds like he might be a rich man."

"Riches aren't what matters," Victoria said, bringing a quiet to the table. She had rich parents but had chosen to stay with the Kinsley family and marry Reese.

A rich man. Josie mulled over the words. If she was to speak to Walker again and say the things she'd planned to say, would he think it was because he was rich? She'd made it plain that she didn't care for poverty.

But as Victoria said, riches weren't what mattered.

What did?

She wished she had an answer.

The day passed, heavy with uncertainty. Dark with disappointment. Full of anxious glances to the west.

It was a good thing she hadn't allowed herself to fall in love with Walker.

It would be even better if she could believe that was true.

But time marched on. Her sisters and their husbands left.

Josie went to bed earlier than usual. It was one way to make the evening pass more quickly.

* * *

MONDAY MORNING, she rose, having had a serious talk with herself. She had plans for her life. Over breakfast, Pa said he would be asking the other board members to come by after supper to count the money and make a few decisions.

As soon as she could get away without leaving Ma and Stella more work than she should, she went to the store.

"Did I get any orders?" she asked Norm.

He held out a sheet of paper. "Lots of them."

She looked at the list. Four women wanted dresses, and ten men wanted shirts. She laughed. A couple of the men had even left their sizes. One of them asked for a red shirt. The other asked for a green one. She looked at Norm's selection of fabric and chose enough to make two shirts.

"If any of these others show up, please tell them to either leave their measurements or come to the manse for me to get them." She took the goods and made her way home.

"Ma, I got fourteen orders."

"You're going to be busy."

"Don't worry. I won't shirk my duties at home."

"Daughter, I never thought you would."

"Ma, if I put a table upstairs, I could do all my work there." It would be so much easier than having to use the kitchen table to cut the fabric.

"Then by all means do so. There's a table in the barn that might do for now."

Ma helped her carry the table upstairs.

Josie scoured it. Made sure there were no splinters to catch and mar the fabric then laid out the yard goods. One cowboy had similar measurements as Pa, so she began with that shirt. A red one. She had pushed the table against the window overlooking the addition. It provided her with good lighting, and if it also allowed her to remember seeing Walker working out there, that was purely coincidental.

That evening the school board counted the money raised by the rodeo. Josie hovered nearby serving coffee and cookies but also waiting to see how successful the rodeo had been.

"It's double what we hoped for," Norm said. "I feel weighed down by having to decide what to order."

"It's more responsibility that I feel we should carry," Pa said. "Why don't we ask for suggestions? Ask people to give their reasons for the titles they would like."

The others agreed, and it was settled.

"Only one problem," Norm said. "We won't likely get the books before the teacher arrives."

"Then let's order some basics. Primers. Classics. That sort of thing. That order should come before the teacher." Everyone agreed to Pa's suggestions.

Josie smiled, wishing she could share the news with Walker.

Didn't it matter to him how successful the rodeo had been? How much people here missed him?

OVER THE NEXT TWO WEEKS, Josie put in long hours cutting, measuring, and sewing. More orders came in. She received payment for the first four shirts and, by the following day, a Saturday, she would have three dresses ready.

Soon she'd have enough for the sewing machine she needed. She'd been discussing it with Norm. He had a catalog, and she'd almost worn out the page as she studied the description over and over.

At 250 stitches per minute, this machine will revolutionize your life.

It was a thing of beauty with gold lettering and detail, mounted on a mahogany stand, with a little handle to turn the mechanism. She couldn't wait to get it.

She hurried back home with more orders and more material.

Besides her sewing she had her responsibilities at home. She promised herself she would not neglect them. There were vegetables to pick and can for the winter. Meals to make. Bread to bake. She helped with the children.

Toward bedtime one evening, Ma caught Josie's arm as she headed upstairs. "I know you're staying up late sewing. I worry you might be overdoing it."

"I'm enjoying the work. Besides, I'm anxious to have enough money to order a sewing machine."

Ma nodded. "First thing I know, you'll be moving into a place of your own just as you've always dreamed." Her smile was a tiny bit uncertain. "That's as it should be, I suppose. So long as you are happy, I am happy."

"Thanks, Ma." Josie kissed her mother on her cheek then went up to her room.

She sat by the window and picked up the dress she had only to hem before it was finished.

Like Ma said, she'd soon have her own place where she would support herself. A home of her own that no one could take away. When she moved out Ma would be able to use this room for a family in need.

It was her dream and had been for many years.

Somehow, she had imagined it feeling better than this.

* * *

WALKER PERCHED on the edge of a cliff, staring out at the rugged mountain scenery. Two weeks he'd been camped there. He had supplies enough for a few more days, and then he would have to decide what to do.

The shock of his uncle-father's announcement had worn off. He'd gone from anger to exhaustion and then numbness. The numbness was leaving his body so that he could now think.

And pray.

How often had he railed against keeping secrets? Look at the harm this secret had done.

But as Josie said, he hadn't handled the truth all that well.

He smiled. Josie. Remembering her face had comforted him through his struggles, but the thought of her watching him ride away, disappointment in her eyes, haunted him.

He directed his thoughts toward sweeter moments. The tender kiss he'd given her. She was ready to tell him about her past when they'd been interrupted. He couldn't imagine that her secret was as powerfully destructive as the one Uncle Paul had delivered, but still, the idea of a secret set his nerves on edge.

For a long time he remained looking out over the landscape as he contemplated his future. He had some hard choices ahead of him.

He guessed the preacher and his wife would be praying for him. Would Josie?

He had spent hours in prayer. What did God want? Why had this happened to him? How could his mother and his uncle have been so sinful? He was the product of their sin. Did that make him a sinful person?

What had Josie said? How did the knowledge of what his mother and uncle did change who he was?

Did she really believe it? Had her opinion of him changed?

The sun was high overhead when he pushed to his feet. He saddled his horse, smiling at the pleasure of getting to know his new mount. Buck liked to make it known he only let Walker ride him because he chose to, not because Walker was boss. But he was a big-hearted horse, ready to tackle the steep climbs required to reach this summit.

Now he guided the horse down the trail. It was almost dark when they reached the grassy hills, and he turned the horse northward.

They rode a few more miles then made camp for the night.

Late the next day he rode under the sign at the gate. 3J Ranch. Walker wondered if it stood for the three Joneses who were supposed to be ranching together. For several minutes, he studied the layout. It was rather extensive. Made the Texas ranch look small in comparison. Front and center stood a big house. From where he sat, it looked like maybe three smaller houses behind. Two barns, sturdy-looking corrals, several outbuildings, a long cabin Walker thought would be a bunkhouse, and a small two-story structure next to it. Uncle Paul seemed to have done just fine on his own.

Walker tried not to feel any bitterness, but it crept through. This was the man who had fathered him, and, because of that act, the Texas ranch had been sold. The Jones family had been broken up.

He hadn't even told his uncle that Ma and Pa had died.

He stopped at the house and waited. Would anyone be home?

The door opened, and Uncle Paul stepped out. "Glad to see you, Walker. Come in. You're just in time for supper."

"We need to talk."

"We can do it over a hot meal."

It had been a long time since Walker had enjoyed some good home cooking but—"Don't remember you cooking."

"You remember correctly. I still don't. I have a man and his wife on the place. The man looks after chores. The wife cooks and cleans, but they have their own house." He jabbed his thumb in a vague direction. "She leaves me to eat in peace while she joins her husband. So, it's possible for us to talk freely."

Seems the man understood there were things that needed to be said that shouldn't be said in front of others. Walker followed him into the house. They were in an entryway that from the lack of coats and boots he knew was reserved for callers. To his right he glimpsed a room with two sofas, four armchairs, a fireplace, and lots of books. To his left, a dining room. Again, it appeared to be saved for special occasions. A wide staircase rose to the second floor.

He followed his uncle down the short hall into a kitchen that took up the entire back half of the house. This, he knew at first glance, was where the ranch life was lived. There was a big table set for one. Cupboards, stove, a desk cluttered with papers, and a doorway that revealed a large boot room.

Uncle Paul put out another setting of dishes. "Sit."

Walker did.

"We'll pray."

Why did that surprise Walker? His uncle had always been faithful in his Christian living. But having committed adultery rather ruined that assumption. Walker was so lost in his thoughts he didn't hear what his uncle said until, "Amen."

They filled their plates and began to eat.

His uncle paused, his fork beside his plate. "Let's get one thing out of the way immediately. I sinned against you, your mother, your father, and God when I did what I did. God has forgiven me according to His word where He says, 'If we confess our sins, he is faithful and just to forgive us our sins, and to cleanse us from all unrighteousness.' I believe His word even when my heart accuses me. I long ago sought forgiveness from your mother, and she said she gave it. I'm hoping that your father can forgive me. Now I'm asking you to forgive me. What I did was wrong, and the whole family paid for it. Walker, can you forgive me?"

Walker put his hands beside his plate. "Uncle Paul." He stopped. "I don't even know what to call you." He couldn't call him Pa.

"Paul will do fine."

"When I left Glory, I went into the mountains to think. I don't mind telling you it was a real shock to learn you are my father." He shook his head. It was still hard to believe. "At first, I was angry. Why didn't someone tell me the truth?"

"I wanted to."

"Then I began to wonder what difference it would have made. What's done is done. The past can't be changed. I want to put it behind me."

Paul pulled his lips down in a gesture of regret. "Unfortunately, some things cannot be forgotten."

"I suppose that's true. But I cannot harbor bitterness in my heart. It will turn me sour. So, I forgive you."

"Thank you." Paul held out his hand and they shook. "I don't mind saying that's a load off my mind." Paul resumed eating. He glanced at Walker. "What are your plans?"

"Thought I'd have a look around and see if this place is as nice as you said it is." He kept his voice neutral, not wanting Paul to think he wanted anything more than a visit. At this point he didn't know what he wanted. "Paul, I have to inform you that both my parents are dead."

Paul's hands fell to the table. "No. When? How?"

Walker relayed the details of his parents' deaths. It seemed his news was as shattering to Paul as Paul's news had been to him.

Paul rubbed his forehead. "I always hoped we'd find a way to resolve things. Now it will never happen."

"We only have today. The past is gone. The future is not yet ours."

Paul smiled. "You sound like your mother."

They nodded, the beginning of understanding between them.

The meal over, they pushed back their chairs and leaned on the back legs. "Now tell me what you've done since I saw you twelve years ago."

Walker chuckled. "That might take a while."

"Good. Let's sit outside on the porch." Paul poured them each a cup of coffee and led the way from the kitchen. The porch faced west. Half a dozen chairs stood on the wooden floor outside. Walker and Paul sat side by side.

Walker started from the sale of the Texas ranch and listed the various jobs he'd had. "I loved working on ranches, but then Pa died. Ma was failing, so I took a job in town at the livery barn."

"Can't see you enjoying town."

Walker shrugged. "Mostly I worked and took care of Ma. Had my horse and went for long rides when I felt I could be away. It wasn't too bad."

The sun lowered in a colorful display. Still they sat outside and talked until Walker couldn't stop yawning.

Paul pushed to his feet. "Looks like it's time for you to go to bed. Come along. I'll show you a room."

Walker followed him upstairs. He was alert enough to see there were five rooms up there. He went into the room Paul indicated, kicked off his boots, dropped his pants on the floor, his shirt on top of them, and fell into bed, instantly asleep.

The next morning, he and Paul rode out to see the ranch.

Three days later, Walker sat across the table from Paul. "It's a nice place."

"Plenty of room for you and a family, if you so desire. I'm not pressuring you though."

Walker chuckled. "You mean pointing out all the beauties of the place and mentioning that you wouldn't mind taking up residence in one of those smaller houses weren't none-too-subtle hints that you'd like me to stay?"

Paul laughed. "I suppose I have been obvious." He leaned forward. "Have you made up your mind?"

"I have to go back and talk to Josie Kinsley. I left in a hurry right when we were in the middle of a very important conversation."

"You go talk to that sweet young gal and convince her she'd be perfectly happy living here."

Walker grinned at the way Paul let him know what he wanted.

Walker left early the next morning.

What had Josie been about to confess to him? He no longer believed that the truth couldn't harm you. Paul's announcement had convinced him otherwise.

Did Josie's secret contain equally distressing news?

There was only one way to find out.

CHAPTER 15

*a*t Pa's request, Josie had agreed to sing a fairly new song by Frances Havergal at the close of the Sunday service. Josie had worked hard at learning the words that drove deep into her heart, challenging her faith.

"Stayed upon Jehovah, Hearts are fully blest; Finding, as He promised, Perfect peace and rest."

As she practiced the song, she knew she had a choice. Trust God for the future knowing He was the Sun of Love who traced joys and trials in her life. Or she could continue to fear and regret the past. She could waste her life thinking of what might have been.

Life could not be lived joyfully and wholly that way.

She knelt at her bed before following her family to church. *God, I don't know what Your plans are for me, but I give my past and its shame to You. I give my future and its uncertainty to You. I give You this day. I will rejoice and be glad in all that Your hand has prepared for me.*

She rose, her heart full of joy, and crossed to the

church, where she stood at the pulpit and nodded to Victoria at the piano. Lifting her gaze above the congregation, she sang the song to her Lord and Savior.

"Those who trust Him wholly find Him wholly true."

She was done. Silence followed the final note. As Pa stood to give the benediction, Josie returned to her seat.

A few minutes later, she made her way down the aisle and outside. And stopped so suddenly, Victoria bumped into her.

"Walker," she whispered. He waited at the bottom of the steps.

His smile was both tentative and welcoming.

Victoria pushed Josie forward. "Go see what he wants."

Josie's feet carried her to his side though she could not remember taking a step. "Will you join us for dinner?" It was not one of the questions begging to be asked, but she was afraid. Afraid of what he might want. Afraid of what she must tell him. *Stayed upon Jehovah*, she reminded herself. Trust His promises. His strength. His guidance.

With her sisters and brothers-in-law ahead of them, she and Walker crossed to the house. She carried serving bowls to the table only because someone placed them in her hands.

She sat in her usual place. Walker sat beside her. She bowed her head. Heard Pa pray but didn't hear his words.

She took food from the bowls passed to her. Walker seemed more able to eat a decent amount than she could.

"Are you back to stay or just to visit?" Flora asked.

"I'll let you know after I have a chance to talk to Josie."

Her teeth chattered so badly she couldn't eat another bite. Someone took away her plate and put a dessert dish before her with a wedge of chocolate cake. She pushed it aside. How could she eat when she didn't know what he would say? Would he remember his promise to settle down and build a home? Had he decided to join his uncle who was his father?

She had no doubt that their discussion would lead to the need for her to be honest with him about her past. And that frightened her.

The meal was over. She carried a stack of dishes to the basin of water and grabbed a rag to wash them.

Victoria pushed her aside. "Walker is waiting. Go with him."

Her limbs feeling like warm butter, she stepped outside, into the bright sunlight.

"Let's go down by the river," he said.

She walked at his side across the dusty road, across the soft grass, through the trees to the bank of the river, and there they stopped.

Walker took his hat off and twisted it round and round in his fingers.

"I didn't know if you'd come back." The words burst unbidden from her mouth.

"Sorry I left in such a hurry. I had a lot to think about." He studied her, his gaze brushing her cheeks, her eyes, her lips.

Was he thinking of the last picnic they'd shared? The kiss he'd given her?

The unfinished conversation? Time to say what she'd started to say.

But before she could speak, he brushed the backs of

his fingers across her cheek. "I went to the ranch. Worked out things with Paul."

What sort of things had he worked out?

She drew in a large breath of air. "Walker, you want truth and honesty. You don't like secrets. Before you say anything more, you need to hear the truth about me."

He squeezed her hand. "As you said to me, your past isn't who you are."

"It plays a large part in who I am now." She met his gaze, found strength in it, and began. "Some of this I have told you, but I have to begin at the start to make sure you understand. My uncle became my guardian when I was young. Too young to know I shouldn't trust him completely, as I'd trusted my parents."

Walker nodded encouragement.

"It took me a long time to realize that he didn't have a job. And the way we survived was by stealing and cheating. At first, I thought it was a game. That's what he said. 'Go in there and ask the storekeeper about the doll. Be sure and look really sad and mention that you're an orphan. Or fall down and pretend you have a bellyache. You do a good job and I'll give you candies.' He taught me how to sneak things and leave the store. Said he would pay for them when he went in. Then one day I got caught stealing a tin of peaches. The store man shook me hard. I can remember his words like it was yesterday. 'You're just a kid so I'm not going to call the sheriff, but I should. You're a good for nothing thief. A low-down skunk. Where's your ma?' I said she was dead. He said, 'Likely she'd turn over in her grave if she knew this was what you were doing.'"

Josie shuddered. "That's when I knew what we were

doing was wrong." She rushed on before Walker could speak. "I have to get it all out."

He nodded.

"I told Uncle I didn't want to do it anymore. He said if I backed out on him, he'd tell the sheriff what I'd done. I was as guilty as he. He scared me into staying with him."

She forced herself to continue. "The worst part was when Uncle woke me in the middle of the night. I remember the first time he did it. I was cold and hungry and angry at him for not taking care of me like he promised Mama. But he clamped a hand over my mouth and told me we had to leave. He didn't even let me pack my things. He just grabbed my coat and shoes and shoved them at me. My heart hammered so hard I thought it would burst from my chest. Uncle led us away from town. Then he jumped into the saddle, and we raced away into the dark. We camped beside a stream just as the sky began to lighten. I was so hungry that I believed him when he told me that people in this area didn't mind if we took what we needed to eat. He told me lots of things that I should have known were lies. But after we had to run away in the middle of the night a few times, I learned to keep my things close. I learned how hunger drives a person to steal. I learned not to believe anything my uncle said."

Her throat grew tight and she couldn't go on.

"How did you end up with the Kinsleys?"

"Uncle saw how his accomplices started to look at me and told me I was getting to be too much trouble. I think he also saw me trying to get up the nerve to speak to the sheriff."

Walker wrapped his arms around her and drew her to his chest.

She leaned into him, finding strength in his embrace.

His voice rumbled beneath her ear as he spoke. "I'm sorry all that happened to you. None of it was your fault. You were a child put in a horrible situation."

"If people found this out about me, they would judge me. It wouldn't be good for my parents and my sisters."

Walker leaned back, caught her chin with his finger, and tipped her head up.

She looked into his clear blue eyes and thought it was like the Montana sky had shared a bit of itself with him.

"Josie, you have no need to carry your past like a heavy load. Tell your parents and your sisters. I think you'll see that they won't condemn you."

"I'm afraid. I've carried this shame so long. I've always been afraid of what would happen."

He kissed the tip of her nose. "You told me, and nothing bad happened."

"It doesn't change how you feel about me?"

He smiled. "Did learning that Paul is my father change how you felt about me?"

"Not at all." At that moment, she understood that she was free of her past, and her shame fell away. She sang softly, "'Those who trust him wholly find Him wholly true.' God loves me and washed away my past." She put her arm through his, and they walked beside the river. "Now tell me what you've been doing since I last saw you."

"I went to visit my uncle...Paul. He has a nice place and wants me to be his partner."

"You've made your peace with him?"

"I have."

"I'm glad." She waited a heartbeat, but he didn't say if he meant to join Paul. She wouldn't ask, afraid he would say he was but not invite her to join him. "Oh, you left before you heard the results of the rodeo. There was enough money for two orders of books. The first one was basics and arrived a few days ago. On the same train as the new teacher. Pa and the others decided to let him have some input into the books they would get with the rest of the money."

"That's great." He paused to study her. "And did you get lots of sewing orders?"

"I surely did." She told him of the first orders. "And every week I get a few more."

"You'll soon be an independent business woman."

"Yes." She had enough money to order the sewing machine, but she hadn't done so. She could not say why, except something held her back. Having almost reached her dream, it no longer felt urgent. She wasn't even sure it's what she wanted.

What did she want?

The thing she had lost when her parents died. Home and love.

But that didn't make sense. Her family loved her, and she had a home with them.

It wasn't enough to satisfy the longing in her heart.

She'd once thought Walker meant to offer her what she wanted.

Had he changed his mind?

* * *

207

WALKER ACHED to tell Josie how he felt, but would she be willing to leave her home? Her plans which were so close to reaching fruition?

Besides, the words of love were pressed back by an anger toward a man who would treat a young girl the way Josie's uncle had treated her. Used her.

"Thank God you ended up with the Kinsleys." It was a complete change of topic from talking about the rodeo and her sewing venture.

"I know." She looked into the distance, a troubled expression on her face. "I need to be honest with them about my past." She turned her steps toward home.

He stayed beside her. He didn't think she needed his presence in order to talk to her family, but he meant to be there.

The girls were gathered outside.

"Where's Ma and Pa?" Josie asked.

"Inside."

"Would you all come in? There's something I want to say."

Their expressions full of curiosity, they all trooped indoors and gathered round the table.

Walker sat beside Josie. He found her hand under the table and squeezed it. She sent him a grateful smile then turned toward her parents.

"First, I want to thank you for adopting me and loving me. If you hadn't, I don't know what would have happened to me. You saved me from an awful life, and I still carry the shame of who I was and what I did. I need to tell you." Her look circled the table. "All of you. I can no longer keep these secrets, and if you change your mind about me, I will certainly understand." Her voice quivered.

"Child, we will never change our mind about you," Ma said. "Unless we are granted the ability to love you more."

Josie sniffed back tears. "Better wait until you hear." Her voice halting, she told her family the same story she'd told Walker.

When she finished, she hung her head.

Her mother pushed back from the table and went to Josie's side. Her pa followed.

"Child, we have known this from the first. The sheriff told us. That's when we determined we would ask your uncle to let us adopt you. You deserved to be free of his control. Never have we blamed you for being part of his life."

Tears streamed down Josie's face as she hugged her parents and was hugged by them.

Her sisters and their husbands crowded around her, insisting they loved her.

Flora said, "If I ever meet this uncle of yours, I will exact justice for how he treated you."

Kade pulled her close. "Let's leave justice to the authorities."

They returned to their seats. Mrs. Kinsley, perhaps seeing that they were reluctant to end the session, made tea and served it with the rest of the cake from dinner.

Flora pushed her chair back. "Well, shoot. When you said you had something to say, I thought it would be that Walker had asked you to marry him and go with him to his new ranch." She gave him a look rife with disappointment.

He pushed his chair back also. "Josie, would you please look at me?"

She turned.

"This might not be the right time or place but—" He fell to one knee. "Josie Kinsley, I love you to the depths of my heart. Will you do me the honor of becoming my wife?"

Tears silvered her face. "You love me?"

"You didn't know?"

"I wasn't certain."

"Answer the man, and put him out of his misery," Flora said.

Josie laughed. "Yes, yes, yes. I'll marry you and follow you to the ends of the earth."

"I'd be happy if you'd just go with me to my ranch."

Amidst clapping and shouts of congratulations, he drew her to her feet and out the door. He thought of going to the river but instead went into the addition. He kicked the door closed behind him then pulled her into his arms.

"Josie, I love you." He kissed her soundly and thoroughly.

Finally, she leaned back. "Walker Jones, I love you. Please don't think it's because you have a ranch and are no longer a penniless cowboy."

He pretended to be shocked. "It doesn't make a difference?"

She wrinkled her nose at him.

He grew serious. "What about your sewing business?"

The smile she gave him warmed him clear through. "It was my way of being safe, but I've learned a very important lesson. It's this. I am safe in God's love and care and with the people He sends into my life to love me."

"I don't mind if you want to run a business."

"I will continue to sew because I enjoy it, but it's no longer so important to me. Now tell me about this ranch of yours."

"I'd sooner do this." He kissed her again.

EPILOGUE

*W*ith the help of her sisters, Josie donned the gray, silk wedding dress she'd made. She had told Walker she didn't want to delay long enough to make it, but he had insisted.

"I don't want any regrets later. Put your best skills to work and fashion a gown you will cherish the rest of your life."

She had kissed him to silence him. "Silly. It isn't my gown I intend to cherish as long as I live."

He widened his eyes. So blue. So full of love and trust. "Really? Then tell me, what is?"

Laughing at his teasing, she'd hugged him. "It's a blue-eyed, handsome cowboy."

Seeing that he meant to pretend he didn't know she was talking about him, she hugged him tighter. "You. Only and always you." She'd learned that his mother's infidelity had made him a little anxious, so she reassured him over and over that she only meant to give her heart once.

"There's only one thing that would make this day more perfect." She glanced out the window.

Eve came to her side. "What would that be?"

"If Tilly and Adele could be here and Josh had been found."

The others joined them. "Josh will be found one day," Victoria said. "If I could be found, anyone can."

"Enough of this." Flora shooed her sisters down the stairs and held Josie's arm to steady her as they descended.

Pa was in the church waiting to marry them.

After some discussion with Walker, they had asked Paul to escort her down the aisle. He'd come at their invitation to meet Josie and the others. In the two weeks he'd visited, Josie had grown to know him and like him. He was a man with deep affections and a noble heart.

"Me?" he'd said when they asked him. "I'm not family."

"Both of us want you to know that you will be a part of our family."

Paul had cleared his throat twice before he answered. "In that case, I'd be honored."

The girls and Paul crossed to the church.

Lisa had agreed to play the piano, and the notes filled the air.

One by one her sisters marched down the aisle.

"Are you ready?" Paul held out his elbow for her to take.

She stepped into the doorway. Pa stood at the front. So did her sisters and their husbands as Walker's attendants. But she saw no one but Walker. His bronzed skin glowing. A white shirt and black jacket making him even more handsome than usual, if that was possible.

The wedding ceremony was familiar. She'd assisted Pa in many of them. The words were likely the same, but she didn't hear them. She saw nothing but the love on Walker's face, heard nothing but the joyful beat of her heart.

After the ceremony, tea was served to the guests. Josie and Walker talked to everyone, received their congratulations. There was no need to hurry away. They had decided to spend their first night in town so they could make the journey to the ranch in one day.

"I can't wait to see my new home," she whispered to Walker.

He'd offered to take her to see it before the wedding, but she'd insisted she didn't care if it was a shack or a palace so long as they shared it.

She nudged Walker. "The sheriff." He was talking to Pa, and they looked her direction. "What does he want? Will I ever get over being nervous when a sheriff shows up?"

He hugged her. "You will. In fact, you might find you like them."

Pa and the lawman came toward them. She grabbed Walker's hand and held on tight.

"Let's find a quiet spot." Pa led them to the kitchen. "I asked the sheriff to do a little investigating, and he has news for you," Pa said.

The sheriff nodded. "I would like to inform you that a man by the name of Obadiah Douglas was arrested three months ago in Ohio. He attempted to escape and was shot. He is deceased. I'm sorry."

Her legs went out from under her, but Walker kept her from falling.

Pa and the sheriff slipped away.

Walker led her to a chair and knelt at her side. "Who is this Douglas man?"

"He's my uncle." She shuddered. "I've always been afraid he would track me down and try and make me work for him again."

"He will no longer be a threat to you."

She smiled though her insides still quivered. "We can start a new life together. The past behind us."

He took her hands. "The future before us." He pulled her to her feet and circled his arms around her. "A life full of endless possibilities." He bent to kiss her.

Just before their lips touched, she said, "Walker Jones, I love you forever and always."

How grateful she was that God had proven to be more forgiving, more generous, more merciful than she imagined and certainly more than she deserved. Indeed, even the bad things in her life had worked together for her good. Bringing her to this place where she was ready to love a man like Walker. God had blessed her with a love that filled every corner of her heart.

ALSO BY LINDA FORD

Buffalo Gals of Bonners Ferry series

Glory and the Rawhide Preacher

Mandy and the Missouri Man

Joanna and the Footloose Cowboy

Circle A Cowboys series

Dillon

Mike

Noah

Adam

Sam

Pete

Austin

Romancing the West

Jake's Honor

Cash's Promise

Blaze's Hope

Levi's Blessing

A Heart's Yearning

A Heart's Blessing

A Heart's Delight

A Heart's Promise

Second-Chance Bride

Reluctant Bride

Prairie Brides series

Lizzie

Maryelle

Irene

Grace

Wild Rose Country

Crane's Bride

Hannah's Dream

Chastity's Angel

Cowboy Bodyguard